Death Rides the Rail

Books by R.G. Yoho

Long Ride to Yesterday

Kellen Malone Series
Death Comes to Redhawk
Death Rides the Rail

Coming Soon!
Death Rides the Rail
Nightfall Over Nicodemus
The Evil Day
Palo Duro
Boot Hill Valley
Return to Matewan
America's History is His Story

For more information
visit: www.SpeakingVolumes.us

Death Rides the Rail

R.G. Yoho

SPEAKING VOLUMES, LLC
NAPLES, FLORIDA
2022

Death Rides the Rail

ISBN 978-1-64540-794-2

I wish to dedicate this book to the brave men
and women of the United States Secret Service.
For those on the President's protection detail,
they risk their lives daily for a man whose political
views may very well differ from their own.
However, they are still willing to take a bullet
to uphold the institution of the presidency,
America's highest elective office.

May our presidents always
be worthy of their sacrifice.

I also want to dedicate this book
to grandchildren, one of the Lord's choicest gifts!

Chapter One

On any other day, the tall man with the blood-stained bandage on his left shoulder might have been enjoying the beauty of this bright, sunny morning. Today, he was looking up at the sky and wondering if he would live to see the nightfall.

The rustlers who had been plaguing the valley for weeks had already killed his horse. Caught in the open as he was, the animal's dead body was his only source of cover. He crouched behind the animal and checked the loads in his six-guns. Desperate to quench his thirst, the man treated himself to one last gulp from his canteen. From the scabbard of his dead horse, he grabbed his Winchester, levered the gun, and chambered a cartridge. Then he waited.

Kellen Malone knew they would be coming soon.

With the man wounded and no longer on horseback, the outlaws figured to have the upper hand. On the other side of the hill, the three mounted riders were planning their final attack on their lone pursuer.

Only one man had ever successfully tracked the three outlaws before and they left his dead carcass as food for the buzzards. Malone had come upon their hideout, the secluded valley where they grazed their stolen horses and cattle. Since the man hadn't brought the law with him, they figured that Malone's death would mean that their location would continue to remain a secret. They almost had him once, wounding the man and leaving him afoot.

"Let's go straight at him, Amos. Ain't no way one man can get all of us."

"Yeah," Jarrett said. "I'm with Dusty. We know the man's hurt. You both saw the blood back there on the trail."

Amos Jenkins spat a stream of tobacco juice on the ground and smiled through his greenish-stained teeth. "Okay, boys! If that's the way you want to play it, then I reckon you can count me in."

As Amos checked his gun, Jarrett reached over and swatted his pal, Dusty, on the back. "This here's gonna be some fun."

***

A heavy set man with a mustache and booming voice just finished speaking to an assembled crowd of citizens on the courthouse steps. The building, fashioned after Philadelphia's Independence Hall, was situated on the town square in Independence, Missouri.

The speaker shook hands with many of those in the crowd and exchanged pleasantries before being ushered to a carriage that would take him to the hotel. An attractive, dark-haired young woman waited for him there.

As he climbed into the carriage, he asked his wife, "How do you think I was received?"

"Fine, dear. It was an excellent address."

"Thank you very kindly, ma'am. You are always a boost to this vain man's spirits!" He pointed towards the jailhouse on the town square. "Do you see that building? Frank James, the brother of Jesse James, was imprisoned there for a time."

"I had no idea. This must have been an exciting place to live!"

The man then nodded at the driver, who gently shook the reins to start the team of horses moving. "Where to, sir?"

"Please take us to the hotel, if you please."

"Yes, sir," the driver said. "It will be an honor."

"So, Frances, how do you like the West?"

"It is like nothing I have ever seen, Grover. Much of it seems to be rather primitive, but the sights and magnitude of the region are nothing short of wondrous."

"You have seen nothing yet. The railroad will take us all the way to Sacramento and you will see some of the most magnificent sights you've ever seen."

"Do you think we will see any Indians?"

"Perhaps, my dear. But most of the renegade Apaches have already been captured or killed. General Miles captured Geronimo some time ago."

The heavy-set man was strangely silent for a time, his eyes staring off towards the horizon. Frances noticed her husband's silence and knew it was out of character for the man. She also noticed these occurrences had become increasingly more commonplace in the last month.

"What is troubling you, dear?"

"It is nothing, Frances. You know how this job can be. The responsibilities of this office can occasionally overwhelm you. There are so many people to please and I am constantly faced with so many weighty decisions. I just want to do the right thing."

"You sure that is all it is?"

"What else could it be?" Grover said with a laugh. He quickly did his best to change the subject. "There is one other thing I've noticed, Frances."

"And what is that?" she asked, as the carriage began to slow down at the hotel's front entrance way.

"I am certainly a long way from New York!"

As the carriage pulled up in front of the hotel, Jeremiah Langston, a short man with a walrus mustache nervously waited next to the front door. A distinguished cavalry veteran of the War Between the States, Jeremiah had worked for the man for the past couple of years.

Langston stepped forward and offered his hand to the lady. "Good evening, ma'am," he said. "May I help you down?"

"Why thank you very much, Mr. Langston."

Frances took Jeremiah's hand and stepped down from the carriage. The woman adjusted her hat and smoothed down her dress. Smiling, Langston reached out and gave Grover a firm handshake.

"It's good to see you too, sir."

Frances turned towards the two men and said, "If you gentlemen will excuse me, I would like to go to our room and freshen up. I can see you both have business matters to discuss, that do not require my presence."

Grover smiled at the woman and removed a cigar from his breast pocket. "I will be along soon, dear. Perhaps we will get a bite to eat then."

"Please don't be too long."

Both of them said nothing further as the woman entered the hotel. Langston took out a match and struck it on the wheel of the carriage. He offered the lit match to Grover, who leaned forward to the flame and took a couple of hearty puffs. Langston took one last look over his shoulder to make sure the woman was actually gone.

"Did you give any more thought to our earlier conversation, Mr. President?"

"Yes, I have. Please walk with me, Mr. Langston?" President Cleveland and Jeremiah walked down the street in front of the hotel. "Do you think the information is credible?"

"Yes, sir, I think so."

"Why would someone want to kill me?"

"Maybe it has to do with your time as sheriff of Erie County. Maybe they don't want you to win reelection. Perhaps they simply do not like you, Mr. President. The reason, I have not been able to determine. But I do believe your life is in danger should you travel westward on the train." Jeremiah placed a hand on the president's shoulder to stop him. "And there is one other thing you need to consider, sir."

"What is that?"

"Your wife, Frances. You have a young bride whose safety you must consider. What if she were to get hurt in an assassination attempt directed on you?"

By this time they had turned around and went back in the direction of the hotel. Before going inside, they stopped to finish their conversation.

"Okay, Jeremiah. You have persuaded me. I suppose I have no choice but to take the threat seriously." President Cleveland stubbed the flaming end of the cigar on the sole of his shoe. Then he tossed it aside. "If you are correct, then there is no way of knowing who might be responsible. Do you know someone who could handle this situation, someone you would trust with your life?" He broke into a smile "Or with mine?"

"Yes, sir, I do," Langston said. "I believe I know just the man!"

***

Kellen Malone heard the rustlers coming before he could see them. Cursing and shooting, the men came charging down the hillside. Still using his dead horse for cover, Kell took careful aim on the lead rider and squeezed off a single shot. The slug hit Jarrett squarely in the chest, sending his body backwards over the rump of his horse.

Now Malone was angry! He wasn't annoyed about the wound on his arm. He wasn't even particularly upset about the death of his horse. Mostly, he was furious that they might actually succeed in their efforts to kill him. Finally with Rachel and his son, he had something worth living for. And he wasn't ready to give it all up because of men such as these.

Although Kell knew they might still kill him, bitterly he decided to make sure at least a couple of them paid for his life with their own!

Dusty's horse was digging its hooves into the dirt, propelling its powerful body down on Malone's improvised fort. Ignoring the bullets that whistled past his face, Kell coolly directed his fire at Dusty. As he triggered the Winchester, the outlaw's horse turned its head into the path of the bullet. The horse went to the ground, throwing Dusty from the saddle. The outlaw skidded across the ground and came up clawing for his gun.

For just a second, Malone was tempted to give the man a fair chance. Second thought told him that he couldn't permit a living outlaw behind him while he turned to face the other one. And after all, it wasn't his choice for them to buy chips in this game. He quickly decided that it was time for all the players to ante up. Before Dusty could fully come to his feet, Kell took aim and dusted the man twice with his Winchester.

Amos Jenkins leaped his horse over Malone and the dead animal. One of the hooves of Jenkins' horse struck a glancing blow alongside Malone's head. It staggered the man and knocked the rifle from his hands. Malone quickly recovered and while still on his back, his hands swept down for his guns. Amos wheeled the horse around and raised his pistol to end the fortunes of anyone who would try to thwart his plans. Triumphantly he smiled at the thought of ending this man's meddling.

His first shot creased the fleshy part of Malone's thigh. It burned like a hot branding iron. Malone winched from the pain, but not enough to still his guns. His twin sixes stabbed flame as Amos readied his second shot. The bullets tore at the outlaw's chest and shoulders. Another shot split Jenkins' ear. The final slug ripped a deadly pass through his lung.

Amos walked his horse forward, no longer trying to lift the gun with his numb, weakened fingers. Harmlessly, the pistol finally fell to the ground. A trickle of frothy blood dripped from the corner of his lip. No stranger to gunshot wounds, the outlaw knew he had only a few brief moments to live.

"Who are you, mister?" he asked, slumping forward in the saddle.

"Kellen Malone."

The man coughed up some more blood. "But I thought you were in jail."

"I got out."

"Ain't that just my luck!" he gasped, just before tumbling off his horse.

***

In a San Francisco office, a trio of powerful men shared some drinks and talked about politics, finance, and the issues of the day. All three of them were leaders in the railroad industry and all were equally concerned about the policies of the president.

Vincent Fielding, a tall, handsome man with chiseled features, glanced around the room at the other executives sitting in this meeting. As the one who assembled this gathering, he did most of the talking. The wealthiest man in the room, Fielding clearly had the most to lose.

"What are we going to do, gentlemen?" Fielding asked. "Cleveland is going to hurt our holdings."

"What makes you so certain that anything will be done about it?" Joseph Blakemore said while stirring cream into his coffee. He stopped to taste it. "You know politicians. They make a lot of promises but seldom follow through with any of them."

"My sources tell me," said Wilson Stonegate, "that currently Cleveland has some people investigating the lands on which we hold government grants."

A portly man of below average height, balding and well-dressed, Joseph Blakemore was an intelligent man who made his fortune from nothing. He scratched out a meager living in the Pennsylvania coal mines, made some connections, and then moved up to management. From there, everything he touched seemed to turn to gold.

"Why should that fact concern me at all?" Blakemore said, his eye glasses continually drifting down toward the end of his bulbous nose.

"One of these Land Office agents stopped by my place the other day," Fielding explained. "He wanted to know why some of the lands I acquired under government grant had been sold to other interests. Don't you think for a moment that they won't be looking into your business next, Joseph! Do you think you can keep your speculative interests in that land a secret forever?"

"I'm not worried about it, Vince. If I need anybody to protect my interests in Washington, then I will simply purchase them. It's always worked before."

Unlike Blakemore's path to riches, Wilson Stonegate became a prosperous man in the span of a single day. An unassuming man with nothing distinctive in his looks and manner, Stonegate grabbed the brass ring when a woman placed a wedding ring on his finger at the church altar. His marriage to a wealthy Presbyterian widow placed him in control of her vast fortune and expanded his prospects beyond his wildest dreams.

"By the way, Vincent," Stonegate said, "I also learned that the agent who came to your place was found murdered the other day."

Despite their association with Vincent Fielding, neither of the other two men could tell you anything substantial about the background of the man. Fielding had obviously accumulated vast sums of wealth, but nobody had any clue as to its origins.

Blakemore and Stonegate knew he had come from somewhere back east. They had even privately hired an investigator to look into Fielding's background. Their efforts proved futile. A report was never issued and the investigator was never seen again.

"I heard that too," Fielding replied sarcastically. He pulled a cigar from the box on the desk, bit off the end, and lit it. "Terrible shame about what happened to the man. Crime just seems to be getting out of hand in San Francisco these days. Perhaps he should have thought about that before he went out alone at night."

"Did you kill him, Vincent?"

"Do I look like a killer, Wilson?"

Stonegate stared at the man silently for a moment. The longer he looked into the railroad executive's eyes, the more certain he was that Fielding had directly or indirectly been involved in the man's death. However, despite those thoughts, Wilson was far too wise to give a voice to his opinion.

Blakemore's question broke up the silence. "So, Vince, how much land are we talking about here?"

"About 81 million acres," answered Fielding. "Our do-gooder President Cleveland thinks we have failed to live up to our grants and obligations on much of this acreage. He wants to take the land away from us by legislative edict or some kind of executive order. In addition to that, the president also wants to assume Federal regulation of the railroad industry."

"I'm getting a little worried about this, myself." Stonegate added. "I worked hard to legally acquire this land from a bunch of poor, stubborn dirt farmers. It wasn't easy. Moreover, I didn't risk my fortune to lay miles of track across a vast prairie, just to see it taken away from me!"

"Legally is a strange word for the way you acquired your railroad holdings," Vince said with a smile. "We all heard the story about those homesteaders outside of Council Bluffs."

"They were all presented with fair and generous offers."

"Until they turned you down," Fielding explained. "Then you burned them out, killed their stock, and chased them naked out onto the plains."

"How dare you say anything about my tactics?" Stonegate blustered. "I understand your methods of operation were much more aggressive, shall we say, than anything I ever did!"

"And what if they were?"

"Gentlemen, gentlemen!" Blakemore interrupted. "We are getting a little off track here. Now is not the time to be fighting amongst ourselves. Our fight is with Grover Cleveland! You're the one who called this meeting, Vince. What do you suggest we do about the president?"

"Yes, that is certainly a good question!" Stonegate added. The sneer on his face was directed at Vincent Fielding. "You are always the man with all the answers. What is your solution to this problem?"

Vincent Fielding smiled like a man who had just taken liberties with his neighbor's wife, another commandment he too had recently broken. "I'm glad you asked, gentlemen. I believe I have come up with a plan that will suit all our needs."

Stonegate looked over at Blakemore and smiled smugly. "It sounds like Brutus is planning to slay the mighty Caesar."

"Very good thinking, Wilson." Fielding said with a chuckle "Perhaps there might be a chance for you to hold onto your wealth after all!"

"Please tell us you're kidding," Blakemore said.

"Friends, Romans, countrymen, lend me your ears! Stonegate is absolutely right about President Cleveland," Fielding said, tossing down the last of his drink. "Oh, he sits high in all the people's hearts, but the man must be overthrown."

Stonegate had already begun to get over his initial shock at the idea. Grudgingly, he could see where the idea had some merits. "Are you sure about this?" he asked.

"Trust me! We are not alone in this venture, gentlemen." Fielding paced back and forth across the room in front of them, like a general reviewing his troops. "I have the backing of several wealthy ranchers and lumber men, all of them the beneficiaries of the railroad's largesse. They have already given their unwavering support of the idea."

"It still sounds a little rash to me," Blakemore observed. He was suddenly whispering like a man conspiring in a crowded diner although there was no one else to overhear them. "I wouldn't even know how to go about carrying out something like this."

"You mean an assassination?" Vincent said the words like he was discussing something as insignificant as the ladies' social hour. "Often in my business dealings, I find it necessary to employ a man who I can trust to carry out my orders—a trouble shooter, if you will."

"You mean a killer!"

"No, Wilson! I mean a trouble shooter. I want you to meet him." Fielding went to the door, opened it, and motioned a man inside. A tall man, smartly dressed in a fine suit and well-polished boots, walked into the room. "Allow me to introduce you, gentlemen. This is Cameron Ellis. He will be our trouble shooter in this matter."

Blakemore and Stonegate were intimately familiar with the name of Cam Ellis. Although neither of them had ever cast eyes on the man, they were both aware of the man's violent reputation. With this man as Fielding's *trouble shooter*, the circumstances surrounding the mysterious disappearance of the Land Office agent suddenly became much clearer.

"Cameron has already begun making preparations for this mission. Above all else, he is a professional and a man of true discretion. Do you gentlemen have any questions to ask our guest?"

"Do you have any idea what you are getting into?" asked Blakemore.

"I don't care what the job is," Cam said, "just so the money's good."

Fielding looked over at Stonegate. "How about you, Wilson? You have anything to ask the man?"

"Yes, I do. Mr. Ellis, we understand that you already know what the job is," Stonegate said, pausing as though he were searching for the right way to phrase his question. "What makes you so sure that you can succeed at this mission?"

Ellis stared at the man like he had just been insulted and challenged to a duel. Inwardly, Stonegate trembled at the killer's response.

"I have never failed at a job yet!" he said proudly. "Don't see anything happening on this one to change that."

As Cameron Ellis looked around the room for any other questions, the scowl on his face and his dark piercing eyes discouraged anyone else from asking them.

"Thank you, Mr. Ellis. You can go now. I will be in touch." Fielding said nothing further until the gunman left the room and the door closed behind him. He turned his gaze on Blakemore, followed by a glance at Stonegate. "Okay, gentlemen. It's decision time. I have every confidence in Cameron Ellis and his ability to complete this assignment!

"Quality help does not come cheap and Cameron has already agreed to my terms. I have contracted with Mr. Ellis for twenty-five thousand dollars. He has already been given fifteen thousand by me. You can wash your hands of all the details. Cameron and I will take care of that. But should you choose to join in this endeavor, then I will need five thousand dollars from each of you."

Before he entered this room, Stonegate had never considered the possibility that he would ever be involved in such a venture. However, he believed the president's actions had left him no other choice.

"Count me in, Vince. Five thousand it is! Cleveland has to be stopped."

"Good choice, Wilson! Now what about you, Joseph?"

"You do know what will happen to us if they catch us, don't you? We'll all hang, just like the ones involved in the Lincoln conspiracy." Blakemore poured himself a shot of whiskey and drank it down in one swallow. He quickly poured another and tossed it down as well. Joseph looked over at Stonegate and then at Fielding. "I can't believe I'm even considering this."

"Joseph, there is one other thing you ought to consider," Stonegate pointed out. "If you're in for a penny, you're in for a pound. Should the particulars of this meeting ever become public, then they will probably hang us all anyway."

"I couldn't have said it better myself," Fielding replied, impressed and surprised by the unexpected clarity of thinking from Wilson Stonegate. "So, Joseph, are you with us or against us?"

Just then, another thought occurred to Blakemore. Fielding's statement sounded almost like a threat. He wondered if Cameron Ellis, Vincent's trouble shooter, was still waiting outside the door to the office. Perhaps there was only one decision he could *safely* reach. And what would be the consequences of turning them down? However, he found the implementation of Cleveland's policies much more frightening than the prospects of Cameron's gun.

"I've been poor once in my life and I didn't like it much," Blakemore said. "I am not going to let this president take what I've acquired or allow him to regulate my business interests! Yes, I am with you, Vince. Five thousand dollars sounds like a small price to control one's destiny."

Fielding smiled as he firmly shook the hands of both men. "You will not be sorry, gentlemen. I will inform Cameron Ellis of your decision. Congratulations! You two men have made history today by plotting the assassination of President Grover Cleveland."

Chapter Two

Sheriff Bill Kimball walked out of the sheriff's office as Kell rode into town with three horses trailing behind him. Each one of the horses had a body tied across the saddle. Still not fully recovered from his bullet wounds, the townspeople had consented to keep Kimball on as sheriff until he was completely healed.

The sheriff immediately noticed the bandage on Malone's arm. "Looks like you had a bad time of it."

"Not as bad as they did." Kell stepped down from the saddle and tied his horse to the rail in front of the office. "They killed my horse and one of my shots killed one of theirs. I had to round up a couple of mounts from the stock they stole in order to get all the bodies back here."

"I'm feeling a lot better now, Kell," the sheriff said with a smile "You could have asked for my help."

"I might have called on you if they had stolen somebody else's stock."

"Doggone you, Kell! I keep telling you that you just can't go around taking the law into your own hands."

Malone smiled. "And I swear, Bill, one of these days I'll take some pains to remember what you told me."

Kimball laughed in spite of himself. "Maybe next time you can stop by the office first, Kell. At least let me deputize you and give you a badge. It might even fool someone into thinking that I actually run a few things back here in Redhawk."

Using a walking stick for support, Kimball gingerly made his way out to the horses to look at the bodies. He moved from one horse to the other, grabbed their heads by the hair, and lifted them up to peer at their lifeless faces.

"These first two I don't know," he said, approaching the third horse. Kimball nodded in recognition at the sight of the last outlaw. "I know this one. His name is Amos Jenkins. Man was a horse thief and a murderer. Got a poster on him in my office. I heard he killed an entire family—women and small children—over near Bisbee."

"Hearing that makes me glad I'm the one who punched his ticket!"

"As I recall," a voice behind him spoke, "you've punched enough tickets to start your own railroad, Mr. Malone."

A smile began to form under the small man's walrus mustache as Malone turned to face the speaker.

"Is that you, Lieutenant?" Malone walked over and firmly shook his hand. "Every time I see you I am reminded that nothing good ever came out of Washington D.C."

"It's good to see you too, Malone."

"Sheriff Bill Kimball, I want you to meet Lieutenant Jeremiah Langston."

The stranger reached out to shake Kimball's hand. "Pleased to meet you, Sheriff."

"The lieutenant," Malone added, "is one of the most incompetent cavalry officers I ever took orders from."

Langston threw back his head to laugh. "Incompetent I will give you. However, you never were any good at taking orders!" he declared. "There wasn't a single order you were ever given that you didn't deliberately ignore or countermand. You got by with it most of the time because you were successful." He directed his gaze towards the sheriff. "Malone was so darned young we didn't know whether to spank him or put him up for court martial."

"Doesn't sound like Kell's changed much!" Kimball said dryly. "He won't pay any attention to me either. What did you do with Kell?"

15

"My superiors finally decided the best course of action was to promote him, pin his chest full of medals, and discharge him."

"Wouldn't have been my first choice, not if you still had a firing squad."

When Malone turned to glare at the sheriff, he saw a smile directed back his way.

"What brings you out this way, Langston?"

"It was good to meet you, Sheriff. Would you please excuse us, sir?"

"No problem, Mr. Langston. I have to figure out something to do with Malone's dead bodies before it gets any hotter out here in the street." He tipped his hat. "It was good to meet you too. My sympathies always go out to anyone who has the misfortune of knowing Kell longer than I have."

During the war, Lieutenant Langston was generally calm under fire. A normal battle never led to any significant change in his demeanor. However, he always got a certain look in his eyes just before a particularly hazardous mission or whenever they were facing vastly superior odds. Kell detected that same look now.

"You look like you could use a drink."

"Only if it's a double shot of whiskey," Langston replied.

"Are things really all that bad?"

"That's what brings me here."

Malone started walking down the street, leading the horse behind him. "The Lady Luck's down the street," Kell explained, "if you're still wanting to get that drink."

Langston shook his head. "Only a confirmed drunkard starts tipping the bottle this early in the day. Besides, I need to talk to you alone."

"Sounds mighty serious, Lieutenant."

"It is, Malone!"

"Are you still working for the president?"

"Yes, I am."

"Where's your horse?"

"Tied to the hitching rail," Langston said with a smile, "in front of the saloon."

"Early in the day—I thought you said…"

Langston cut Kell off before he could finish the sentence. "I didn't say I wasn't a drunkard; I just confirmed that I know what one is."

As Malone and Langston rode out of town, they swapped dozens of lies and laughs. The two Army veterans spoke of old times and battles past. They recalled the brave and noble men they served with during the war, and the gallant souls who never returned from it.

As is often the case, the men serving in uniform form a special brotherhood. The heat of battle often forges bonds that are stronger than those borne of blood. These two men had faced some of the worst fighting of the war and lived through it. Their shared experiences made them closer than brothers."

Langston marveled at the wide skies and rugged beauty of the land stretched out before him. Momentarily he forgot about his reason for coming west.

"You know, Kell. This is my first time to visit this part of the country. After seeing it, I am sorry I waited so long."

"Yes, it's something to see! While I was in Yuma, I feared I would never again see it from atop a horse.

"I almost forgot about your time in prison."

"You know about that, do you?"

"Yes, I do, Kell. We know all about you. We know all about the circumstances concerning your imprisonment. We know about your work for General Nelson Miles. We also know that your name was eventually cleared of any wrongdoing." Langston paused to lean on his saddle horn. "We even know how you deliberately destroyed government evidence that could have convicted your friend Joe Clements, a hired killer." Jeremiah smiled before he continued. "It was that revelation that convinced me you were still the reckless, impulsive, resourceful, and daring young man who I was only occasionally proud to command."

"Who knows about me besides you?"

"The President of the United States."

Malone was skeptical. "Why would President Cleveland care about a former convict turned rancher who lives clear across the country in Arizona Territory?" Finally he could no longer contain himself. "So, tell me," Kell said. "What brought you out here? I know you didn't come all this way for the scenery."

"I need your help."

"My help? What would a man working for the president need me for?" Kell stopped his horse, removed his hat, and wiped his brow with the sleeve of his shirt. "I don't know anything about politics or diplomacy."

"You're right about that!" Langston blustered. He threw back his head and roared with laughter. "No, Malone, we'll leave those things to someone else. What we need from you is exactly the opposite of diplomacy."

"Meaning what?"

"I am intimately familiar with your proficiency with a gun, Malone. After seeing the three dead bodies you left with the sheriff, I am now certain that you have lost none of your skills." Langston looked around to make sure nobody else was in earshot of them. "What I have to tell you, Malone, must remain a secret. Can you do that?"

Now it was Malone's turn to laugh. "Did you ever find out about my disobedience to your orders until the battles were over?"

"I certainly can't argue with that." A solemn look came to the man's face. "There have recently been some threats on the president's life."

"Sorry to hear that, Langston. From what I've heard of the president, Cleveland sounds like a good man. But what do these threats have to do with me?"

"I want to hire your services, Malone. I trust you and I need you to protect the president's life."

Malone shook his head. "There's nothing I can do for you, Lieutenant. You know I don't have any use for Washington."

"Washington? Who said anything about Washington?" Langston removed a map from his saddlebags, opened it so Kell could see, and pointed towards the president's westward route. "President Cleveland is going to be traveling from Omaha to Sacramento. I want you to protect him while he's on the train."

Kell looked up from the map. "Who is trying to kill him?"

Langston paused long enough to tuck the map back into his saddlebags. "That I don't know yet. We do have reason to believe the threat is credible and that someone has been contracted to assassinate the president."

"It sounds like a big job."

"That is not a problem, Malone."

"Not a problem for you, Langston," he said with a laugh. "It might be for me, especially when I'm jumping in front of bullets meant for Cleveland."

The man with the walrus mustache smiled. "That's not what I meant. I meant that we are prepared to pay you ten thousand dollars to protect the president. In addition to that, we'll even let you choose your own team."

"Team, you say? I thought you wanted to keep this thing quiet. The more people you have involved in something, the greater the chances are that word will leak out."

"That is why we want your discretion, Kell."

"Then let me get this straight. You want me to protect the president and I can pick the men I need to help me. Is that correct?"

"Yes, sir."

"Then I'll need Joe Clements."

"Are you crazy, Malone? I said discretion, not disaster! Skull Clements is an outlaw and a killer, not the kind of man in whom I would trust the president's life!"

"But I'd trust him with mine!" Kell exclaimed. "That's all that matters."

"No, Malone. It's out of the question."

"Okay then!" Malone said before spurring his horse down the trail.

Silently, Langston stared after him. Then he desperately urged his horse onward, struggling to catch up with the man.

"Wait, Malone!" he yelled. "Is that your last word on the subject?"

"Is that yours?"

Malone slowed his horse some and Langston finally caught up to him. He reached out to catch the reins of Kell's horse. "Hold up a minute, Malone. Please?"

"I didn't figure there was anything else for us to talk about. Clements is a deal breaker with me, Langston"

He stared Kell directly in the eye. "The man is a gunman for hire, Malone. Are you telling me that Skull Clements' past doesn't give you pause?"

"No, it doesn't. In fact, it makes him an even better man for the job!"

"How do you figure that?"

"Clements knows exactly what it takes to track down a man and kill him. For that reason alone, I can't think of anybody better at also knowing how to prevent it."

"I suppose you make a good point."

"One other thing you ought to consider. If President Cleveland is the target of a gunman, and if guns are needed to defend his life, then I want Joe Clements fighting there alongside me!"

"After listening to your reasoning I've changed my mind, Malone. I think I now like the idea of having Clements on our team. But it's not for the reason you think."

"What do you mean?"

"Even you admit that Skull Clements sells his gun for money and he's quite good at his vocation," Langston said. "Has it ever occurred to you? With his skills, the assassins might be interested in hiring Clements too."

Langston continued riding on down the trail while Malone fully contemplated the words the former military officer just said.

"Not bad thinking," he muttered under his breath. Malone nodded his head in grudging approval. "Not bad at all, Lieutenant."

***

As the tall man walked into the saloon in Denver, he stopped just inside the swinging doors to let his eyes adjust to the change in lighting. Then he looked down at his clothes and noticed that they were covered with trail dust. He attempted to brush it away with his hat before making his way over to the bar.

The room was quite full for this time of the evening. The man generally sought to avoid crowds, but this could not be helped. Joe was to meet someone here about a job and he figured he had earned himself a beer while he waited.

Spotting an empty place in the crowd of patrons, Joe made his way over to the bar. He nodded at the barkeeper. "I'll have a cold one," he said.

As Joe waited for the bartender to return, he leaned his elbows on the bar and stared straight ahead in the mirror. Carefully, he checked out the faces in the crowd behind him. He didn't see anyone there he recognized.

A couple of men were drinking at the bar just to his left. The man beside Joe had obviously had too many. Laughing wildly at something his friend had just said, he backed into Joe and spilled his drink.

"Why don't you look where you're going, mister?" he said to Joe.

"Sorry about your drink," Joe said. "But you're the one who backed into me."

The friend of the angry, drunken man put his hand on the man's shoulder. "Just let it go, Pete. The guy didn't do nothing."

"You might let it go, but I'm not going to!" he said, tossing his shoulders to loose his friend's hand. "Somebody needs to teach this hombre some manners."

"Thanks, anyway." Joe said, his green eyes turning cold. "But I had a momma and pa for that. Don't suppose your momma ever knew who your pa was."

"Well, what's that mean?" he asked, his hand twitching just above his gun butt.

"It just means I know something about manners, friend. That's why I'm willing to forget this whole thing and buy you another drink, to make up for the one you dropped. How about it?"

"I don't think so," he said, backing down the bar to put some distance between them. The man looked like he was ready to draw.

Joe turned to face him.

The other customers in the saloon immediately saw that this could become a shooting situation. Quickly they began to clear the two men a path along the bar.

"Don't do this, Pete!" his friend pleaded.

"No! You shut up! This man is asking for it."

Disinterested, Joe's green eyes merely stared at the man. "It's still not too late for me to buy you that drink, friend."

"Friend—he calls me. You hear that, Coley? This stranger's about to piss his pants."

"You're the one who ought to be pissing your pants! Look at him close, Pete." Coley explained. "You see that scar on his cheek? That's Skull Clements, the gunman!"

"Skull Clements? So what! The man's probably never killed anyone facing him."

"Now's your time to find out," Joe said.

"Well, I ain't gonna let you back out of this one, Clements. Draw your gun now!"

Pete's hand swept down for his gun. Before his fingers touched the butt of his pistol, Joe's six-gun was already out and leveled at his belly.

Quickly and deliberately, Clements walked up on the man. With his other hand, he viciously slapped Pete across the face. The force of the blow nearly lifted the man from his feet. Then he slapped him again.

"Listen to me, you drunken fool. The next time you plan to draw on a man, you better make sure you take the thong off your shootin' iron first!"

Pete's face turned ashen as he looked down at his gun.

"You," Joe said, motioning at Coley with his gun. "What's your name?"

"Coley Simpson."

"Okay, Coley Simpson. Why don't you do your friend a favor and help get him out of here? Maybe give him a chance to sober up."

"Yes, sir." Coley replied, half leading and half dragging his friend out the doors of the building.

All activity in the saloon ceased as the bitter conversation between Clements and Pete built to an eventual climax. Silently, the crowd watched the two men leave the saloon. Once they exited the door, the conversations resumed, quickly followed by the sounds of laughter and the clinking of glasses.

"That really shines, mister!" the bartender said to Clements. "You had the drop on that man. You could have just gone ahead and killed him. The drink's on me, friend."

"Thanks, Barkeep."

Despite Clements' scar, one of the saloon gals was quite taken with the green-eyed gunman. Her experiences in this world rarely left her astonished about the actions of a man; however, even she was surprised that he had chosen to let the drunken man live.

Hoping Joe would buy her a drink, the red-haired saloon girl walked up to the bar and gently brushed up alongside the quiet gunman.

"Hi there, stranger. I'm Jenny Edwards."

"Pleased to meet you, Jenny Edwards. I'm Joe Clements," he said, gently tipping his hat to the woman.

Still under the influence of too much liquor, Pete's wounded pride quickly overruled his normally good judgment. Now he wanted revenge. Pushing aside his friend's hand and drawing his gun, Pete swayed from side to side. Coley caught him again; but as before, Pete shook himself free.

Then he started a crazed, drunken rush towards the saloon doors. From there he leveled his gun at the back of the scar-faced gunman.

As Clements started to ask the bartender to bring the woman a drink, from the corner of his eye he saw the glint of a gun barrel over top of the swinging doors.

In order to get the woman safely out of the line of fire, Joe pushed her aside with his left arm. At the same moment, his right hand grabbed iron. Clements placed a couple of shots through the swinging doors, leaving two bloody eye prints on the man's chest.

The slugs from Clements' gun caused Pete to fire wildly and his bullet harmlessly lodged itself in the hardwood of the bar. He staggered forward and tumbled face-first onto the floor of the saloon.

Coley followed him into the place, his hands held high in the air, so as to pose no threat. As the man hurried inside, Clements had immediately swung his gun around to cover the drunken, back shooter's friend.

"I didn't have anything to do with that, Clements. I swear!" his friend exclaimed, kneeling by Pete's now lifeless body. "I tried to stop him."

Seeing nothing but truth in the man's eyes and statement, Clements holstered his gun. "Sorry I had to kill him. He didn't leave me a whole lot of choice."

"I know that, Clements. Pete was the best friend a man could ever have when he was sober; but he was always a fool when he drank."

Clements hung his head. "Then I am truly sorry for your sake, friend."

A couple of men stepped from the crowd and helped to carry Pete's body from the room. Somebody else threw some sawdust over the blood stained floor. As Coley started to follow the men carrying his friend's body outside, he turned back towards the gunman.

"Thanks for your kindness, mister. You'd be welcomed at my fire anytime."

"Same here," Clements replied, with a quick tip of his hat.

As the danger was now passed, the saloon girl's attention returned to the man who fearlessly shoved her out of the path of a bullet. She walked up beside him again.

"That was a brave thing you just did, Mr. Clements," she said. "A man is desperately trying to kill you and your first impulse was to protect me. Thank you."

"It was my pleasure, Miss Jenny," Clements said with a smile. "And the name's still Joe. I couldn't live with myself if I let the most handsome woman in this town get herself killed."

This woman who had rarely blushed in years suddenly felt her face growing red. Jenny's tainted past often left her feeling that she was entitled to nothing other than rude words and vile talk, the drunken pawings of cowboys too long on the trail, or the amorous attentions of men whose wives were generally unaware of their proclivities.

"That is so kind of you to say."

"I'm not in the habit of saying things I don't mean." Clements turned towards the bartender. "Get Miss Jenny a drink of whatever's her pleasure."

"Thank you, Joe."

"You're welcome, Miss Jenny."

"I believe I will have a beer with the gentleman," she said to the bartender.

"Thanks, Barkeep," Clements said, as the man brought their drinks. He then tossed some money on the bar. "Ma'am, would you care to sit for awhile?"

"I think I would like that."

They picked up their drinks and moved to the back of the room. Seeking little more than a few moments of polite conversation, this lonely pair of wounded individuals hunted a table in the back of the room. Both of them had been injured in this life, one with a scarred face and the other with a scarred soul.

"Skull Clements?"

The speaker was a well-dressed man who looked rather out of place in this meager saloon. One glimpse told Clements that it had been a long time since this man spent any time away from the distant world of silver, china, and fine place settings.

"Yes, some people call me that."

"I believe you told me to meet you here. My name is Vincent Fielding. I think we have some business to discuss."

Clements looked disgusted for this sudden interruption. His eyes drifted from this man to the pleasant redheaded lady waiting to share his table.

"Would you please excuse me for a couple of minutes, Miss Jenny? Just take that table over there. And I assure you, this won't take long!"

"Okay, Joe. Please take your time."

Fielding said nothing further until the woman took her place at the table. He removed a watch from his vest pocket and checked the time.

"You got somewhere to be?"

Fielding ignored the comment. "Do you care to sit down, Mr. Clements?"

"No, I don't, Mr. Fielding. Now why don't you hurry up and get down to your proposal."

"My associates have told me about your skills with a gun. Now that I've seen you in action, apparently those reports were not exaggerated."

"How nice."

"Mr. Clements, I need your help eliminating a problem."

"That's funny. Most people only want me around for my outstanding table manners."

Now it was Fielding's turn to look disgusted. He wasn't used to people talking to him with such insolence. He might have dealt with it more harshly, had he still been back in his own environment.

With Jenny watching from across the room, they continued talking for several minutes. Finally, the well-dressed man nodded at something Clements had just said. He reached into his pocket and handed Joe a thick, cash-filled envelope.

Joe looked inside the envelope and flipped through the stack of bills. "Lot of money for killing a man," he said, softly. Then his eyes returned to the lady, smiling at him, waiting for Joe to join her at the table.

"Well, will you take the job, Mr. Clements?"

"Thanks, Fielding," he replied, handing the cash-filled envelope back to the man. "But I think I just had a better offer."

"A better offer?"

Joe directed his gaze over towards the woman.

"I understand, Mr. Clements. Perhaps another time."

"I don't think so, Fielding."

"What do you mean by that?"

Joe simply smiled at the man facing him. "I can't exactly put my finger on it. Guess there's just something about you that I don't like."

Although he was greatly angered by the gunman's statement, Fielding's face revealed none of his resentment. Saying nothing further, he rose and quickly left the saloon.

Disinterested, Clements watched him go. He did take special note of the tall man in black, who only left his spot at the bar when Fielding walked outside. Something about the man looked vaguely familiar to him. Joe puzzled over it for a minute and then turned back towards the woman.

Only then did he smile.

Clements walked back over to the woman's table, removed his hat, and took a seat beside her. "Sorry about that, Miss Jenny." Gently placing his tough, weather-beaten hand over top of hers, he said, "Now where were we?"

Chapter Three

Silently, Kellen Malone stared out the window at the landscape. Like a canvas that was continually changing before him, he admired the trees, rocks, and hills they passed on their way eastward. A vast number of Hereford cattle were grazing on a hillside, their red bodies and white faces, a striking contrast with the green grass and the blue skies.

Then he directed his gaze to the lovely auburn-haired woman, whose head rested on his shoulder. Kell gently placed his rough, weather-calloused hand on hers.

Rachel Malone stirred from her slumber. "I must have dozed off."

"Sorry I woke you."

"I'd slept long enough. Besides, I'd rather spend some time with you."

"Train should be stopping in another hour."

"Good. It will be nice to walk around some." Rachel paused to stare off at the horizon. "Bill told me about it, you know."

"Told you about what?"

"About you bringing in those rustlers."

"Sheriff Kimball talks too much!"

"And you don't talk enough. He said you could have been killed."

"I could have been killed, if a horse threw me on the way to town. I could have been killed in the war. I could have been killed, if lightning struck me out on the range. Life's a dangerous thing, Rachel. And it's certain nobody gets out of it alive."

"Don't change the subject, Kellen Malone! I'm not telling you to change who you are. I'm also smart enough to know that you wouldn't listen anyway." She reached out and softly took his rough, weather-beaten hand. "I just want to know about everything. Don't hide the dangers from me, Kell. After what we've been through, I can take it. All I'm asking is for you to keep me informed and let me face it with you."

Kell leaned forward and kissed her fully on the lips.

"You are an extraordinary woman, Rachel Malone."

"Yes, I am. It would take an extraordinary woman to put up with you." The smile on her face faded and was quickly replaced by a look of concern. "Now tell me what we are doing here. You didn't just suddenly decide to take a little trip on a private coach."

Kell knew the two of them were alone, but he still took a quick glance around to make sure nobody could hear them. He paused for a moment, trying to find the words to explain the situation. At the same time, he wondered how much he should tell her. But he also knew that anything he shared with Rachel would be kept in strictest confidence.

"We are on our way to meet the president."

"The president," she muttered. "President of what?"

"The President of the United States."

Rachel said nothing, as the sudden realization of what her husband said began to finally have its full effect.

"Do you remember Jeremiah Langston, the man who came to the ranch?"

"You mean the lieutenant you used to serve with in the army?"

"Yes. That was him. Langston works for President Cleveland."

"What does that have to do with you?"

"Langston believes someone is trying to kill the president. He wants me to protect the man and keep anything from happening."

"Then, we're on our way to Washington?"

"No. President Cleveland is taking the train to Sacramento. I plan on meeting them in Omaha, Nebraska."

"Then why am I here?"

"Rachel, nobody knows who may be behind this plot. Langston and I thought it best to get you away from the ranch while I was gone. I'm a little concerned about your safety by having you here, but I'm a lot more scared of what might happen if I left you behind at home."

"What could happen at the ranch?"

"If these people trying to kill the president found out I was protecting him, they might use you to get me out of the way."

"Then they don't know you like I do," she said with a laugh and a squeeze of his hand. "The Kellen Malone I'm married to wouldn't ever betray a friend or leave any kind of a job unfinished."

"So, you think you know me, huh?"

"No, but I'm learning. And every day I find myself looking forward to another day in the classroom."

"All this time I've been promising to take you somewhere, Rachel," Kell said as he took another look out the window. "Just sorry it had to be under these circumstances."

"You just hush your mouth, Kellen Malone. I'm happy to be finally spending some time with you away from the ranch."

"But like I told you, it could be dangerous."

"All the more reason for me to be here with you."

"I didn't mean dangerous for me. My point is that it could be dangerous for *you*."

"Isn't it dangerous for you too, Kell?"

"I can take care of myself."

"I know you can. And you can take care of me too. I know that." She smiled at the tough, but gentle man who was now her husband. "That is why I am happy to be here with you. And besides, we never really did have a honeymoon."

Kell smiled. "For me, every day spent with you *is* a honeymoon."

"You smooth talker, you. But don't think for a minute that talk's going to get you out of buying that dress you promised me."

***

As the train whistle sounded outside Omaha, a tall man with green eyes checked his watch. One side of his lip turned up in a smile. The train was keeping good time. He was glad he hadn't chosen to linger at the restaurant long enough to enjoy that third cup of coffee. Fearful of missing the train, he wanted to arrive promptly.

"You take good care of my horse," he said to the hostler at the stable, "and I will make it worth your trouble when I return."

"Yes, Mr. Clements."

"The name's Joe, son."

"Okay, Joe."

The young man's eyes grew as large as saucers as the quiet, scarfaced gunman thumbed off several bills in the young man's hand.

"I want him well-cared for, you understand?"

"Yes, sir. You can count on me, Joe."

Clements removed his saddle bags and tossed them over his left shoulder, flashing him an easy smile. "I always could recognize a good man," he said before turning to go.

The boy squeezed the greenbacks tightly and shouted after him. "Don't you worry about him none, Joe. Your hoss'll be here when you get back."

As Joe left the stable, he checked his jacket pocket to make sure he still had the ticket for the train with him. He picked up his pace as he headed up the street towards the train depot. He knew Malone would be somewhere on the train waiting for his arrival.

Increasingly, he found his thoughts returning to Jenny, the sweet, red-haired saloon girl that he chanced to meet in a Denver saloon. Ever since the death of his Sioux wife many years ago, Clements had never felt quite the same way about another woman…

Until now.

In fact, after meeting the saloon girl, Joe had passed up several lucrative job offers. He had even chosen to stay in Denver for almost a month, about three weeks longer than he had remained in any single town for half a year. Knowing Jenny even made him think about giving up the business and looking for some other line of work.

Yet he wasn't cut out to run a store. And unlike Kellen Malone, he had no interest in ranching. All that Clements ever knew was a gun.

To Joe Clements, the six-gun had always been a means to survival and his only logical vocation.

There certainly weren't a lot of professions clamoring for a man with his particular sort of skills. However, he had recently begun to toy around with the idea of becoming a small town marshal. Perhaps he could find a sleepy, out of the way place. Maybe he could put down roots somewhere, a quiet little community where folks might not be familiar with his name.

He knew it was unlikely.

With that distinctive scar on his face, Joe knew he could no more escape his reputation than Adam's son could escape the mark of banishment that God placed upon him after killing his brother, Abel.

"Good afternoon to you," the black train porter said to Clements. "You have any bags to load, mister?"

"No, sir," Clements replied with a smile. He paused to firmly shake the man's hand. "But thanks anyway."

The porter smiled, tipped his hat, and opened his hand to reveal the silver dollar that Clements had placed there.

"Thank you kindly, sir!"

Preparing to step onto the train, Joe reached for the railing. He stopped at the sound of a voice behind him.

"Skull Clements!"

"The name's Joe!" Clements said as he turned to face the speaker. He didn't like what he saw when he turned around.

The man who spoke up had a gun pointed directly at Joe's midsection. This lean, wolfish figure was not alone. Two other men also had the drop on Clements. One was off to the speaker's left. The other one was at Clements side, standing alongside the friendly, black porter.

"You killed my brother just outside town a while back!" he said. The man spoke loudly, in order that everyone waiting to board or exit the train might hear what he had to say. "Now I am going to kill you."

The crowd around them did one of three things. Most of them froze in fear; others quickly departed; or some just ducked into the safety of the train station.

"This man is Skull Clements, a notorious gunman. Last month, he shot my brother down in cold blood."

"But I've never even been to…"

The man cut him off before he could finish the sentence. "You shut your trap, Clements! I aim to kill you for what you done to my brother."

Joe knew that the jacket that hid his gun was likely to slow his draw. He also knew it was probable these men would succeed at killing him. But at that very moment, Clements coolly determined that, even if he was injured, he would live long enough to kill the liar who braced him. His green eyes turned cold.

The porter wasn't generally used to the special kindness that Clements directed his way. Mostly, he was greeted with insincere gratitude, apathy, and contempt.

Just as the wolfish man pulled a trigger on the gun he was pointing at Clements, the black porter struck the gunman next to him with some patron's carpetbag. The force of the blow knocked his gun off target, sending a bullet into the floor at Joe's feet.

Suddenly distracted by the activity next to the train, Clements' accuser failed to see Joe go for his gun. Realizing Clements was drawing his weapon, the man fired too fast and missed. His shot struck the train as Joe squeezed off his first shot.

The bullet struck the man low and hard, turning his body out of the path of Joe's second shot. Desperate to live and seeing images of Jenny, Clements' mind was focused on nothing other than killing the man in front of him.

The two men exchanged gunfire.

The porter, desperately trying to escape the path of flying bullets, had dived on the ground, covering his head with both hands.

The other gunman, who had been knocked off balance by the baggage handler, had finally regained his footing. He started to shoot the black man, decided against it, and brutally kicked the porter in the ribs. Then he turned his fully-loaded gun on Clements' unprotected flank.

At that same moment, another armed man stepped out from the shadows. He had only gotten off the train briefly to send a couple of telegrams. After finishing his business, the sounds of shooting had drawn his attention.

The man was Kellen Malone.

Malone quickly palmed his gun and triggered one quick shot at the third gunman. Striking its victim in the head, Kell's slug killed him instantly. Then he turned his gun on the man at Joe's side.

Immediately realizing the new threat that was directed his way, the man turned to face Kell. With an ugly sneer on his face, he fired much quicker than Malone expected. The slug burned a path along Malone's side, leaving a bullet hole in the coattail of his new suit.

Kell's first two shots, the percussions coming as one, struck the man just to the left of his heart and the other one, two inches down from that. The slugs sent his body backward into the train. As he collapsed to the ground, he left a bloody streak down the side of the railroad car.

Conscious that some mysterious benefactor had removed the other two threats, Joe's green eyes blazed. His six-gun put three more shots into the man who falsely accused him of killing his brother.

The man, game until the end, raised his gun one last time. With his last conscious moments, he desperately tried to kill the man he was paid to execute. The gun fell from his then-weakening fingers.

"We had you cold," he muttered.

Then he tumbled onto his face in front of the train.

Gun firmly in hand, Malone surveyed the damage and looked for any other threats. Seeing none, he punched out the empties and started to reload.

"Thanks for the help," Clements said.

"Glad I could help."

"Not you, Kell," he said with a smile. "I was talking to the porter."

The black man had come to his feet and was busy brushing the dust from his clothes. He smiled at the gunman.

"Just glad I could return the favor," he said while picking up Joe's dropped saddlebags. "Here you go, mister."

"Thanks again."

Joe took them and returned them to a spot over his left shoulder. Then he stepped forward and shook Kell's hand.

"The town here was pretty peaceful until you arrived. Can't you go anywhere without stirring trouble, Kell?"

"It wasn't me they were trying to kill."

Just then, one of the men working at the train depot came rushing up the boardwalk, with the sheriff in tow.

"This is him," he said, pointing at Clements. "This is the man who shot that fellow's brother in cold blood last month, Sheriff. I heard the dead man say so."

"Just cause someone said it, don't make it so, Ben. I once heard a man say he wrassled a tornado, but it didn't make it true. This town ain't had no killings in over six months, lessen you count Old Man Dawkins, who was thrown from his horse while in a drunken stupor. But come to think of it, that might have been a murder, especially the way the old man beat that horse whenever he was drinking."

Silently, the sheriff looked at the man with the scar on his cheek. Then he turned over the man's body with his foot.

"You kill this man?"

"Yep."

"I killed the other two," Kell added.

The sheriff studied the dead man's wounds and then looked once again into the green eyes of Joe Clements.

"That was some good shootin'."

"Glad you approve, Marshal."

The railroad conductor shouted, "All aboard!"

"Guess you're free to go, Clements. Same goes for you," he said, looking at Malone. "Go on. Get out of here!"

***

From the window of a passenger car, a man dressed in black gently pulled aside the curtain. Silently, he studied the bodies and bloodshed littering the train depot. After taking in the entire scene, he shook his head in disgust.

"I told him those guys weren't good enough for the job," the man muttered under his breath. "Maybe next time, they'll listen to me."

Then he gently let the curtain fall back into place.

***

Fearful of the sounds of gunfire, Rachel threw herself into the arms of Kellen Malone as he entered their private car. She passionately kissed him out of fear and relief.

"Wow," he said. "That's quite a welcome."

"I'm so glad you are okay, Kell. I heard the shooting."

"Got into a little shooting scrape, but I'm all right, Rachel."

Then the woman viciously slapped him across the arm. "Don't you scare me like that again, Kell."

"I'm sorry. Three men tried to ambush Joe."

"Is he okay?"

Just then, Clements entered the car behind them. "Yes, I'm fine."

She immediately made her way over to Kell's friend and hugged him gently.

"It's so good to see you again, stranger."

Despite his obvious embarrassment, Joe kissed her softly on the cheek. "It's good to see you too, Miss Rachel."

"You left rather suddenly," Rachel said. "Kell and I never even had the chance say our goodbyes. Why did you leave?"

"What kind of question is that to ask a man?" Kell blustered.

"It's okay, Kell," Clements said with a smile. "How else is a woman supposed to glean information? I guess you could say being a lawman was getting a little too respectable for me. Hard thing for a man to live up to. Here lately, I've been in Denver."

Rachel walked over to the table, turned over a clean glass, and poured Clements some brandy. She carried it over to the man. "This time in Denver, was it business or pleasure?"

Once again, Malone thought the question was too intrusive. "Rachel."

The woman's response brought a smile to both the men.

"I'm just gleaning information."

Out of anybody else, this question to Clements would have been taken as a rude intrusion into his business. And rude intrusions into the man's business were usually occasions for fists or gunfire. Joe was equally adept with both. He just preferred the gun. Out of Rachel, the question was merely the kind concern of a good friend.

Normally tight-lipped, Clements was always amazed by the personal information that Kell's wife could routinely get out of him. Malone was fascinated by her abilities, as well.

Perhaps Joe had a soft spot for Rachel because she reminded him of his dead wife. Maybe he was only tolerant of the woman because of his friendship with Malone and her relationship to him.

"It started out as business, Miss Rachel. But in the course of my business, I met a woman there. Her name is Jenny."

"I am so happy to hear that, Joe. A good man like you shouldn't be alone."

"A good man, you say," Joe said, laughing softly at the phrase. "First time anybody ever called me that."

"Now just you stop it, Joe. I won't have you talking that way about yourself."

Like a kid scolded by his mother, Joe muttered softly, "Yes, ma'am."

"Joe, did you happen to know any of those men who tried to kill you?" Kell asked. "Was there anybody who looked familiar to you?"

"Never laid eyes on them before today," Joe replied, grateful that someone had finally changed the subject away from his personal life. "By the way, I never thanked you for your help. How did you happen to be out there, anyway? I expected you to be waiting on the train."

"I was sending a couple of telegrams. Rachel has asked me to be careful," he said with a smile. "That was why I figured this job was big enough that we needed some more help. When I stepped out the door, there they were bracing you."

"They had me dead to rights."

"Maybe, but I was certain you'd would kill at least one of them, if not two. I've seen you in action before."

"I still appreciate your help."

"You'd have done the same for me."

"Are you sure of that?" Clement said with a look of feigned seriousness. Then he began to smile. "Since coming here to get this job nearly already got me killed, maybe you want to go ahead and tell me what it is."

"Aren't you going to ask me about the money first?"

"Not with you, Kell. If you're in, then you can count me in."

"They're paying you five thousand dollars, Joe. They've offered me ten. So, here's what I'll do," he said. "I'll keep five grand of their money and split the other five with you. Does that sound fair to you?"

"It sounds to me like they aren't real good judges of gun talent," Joe said, with a laugh. "They're paying you way too much. But who do I have to kill?"

Kell and Rachel both laughed.

Joe looked bewildered. "What did I say?"

"You don't have to kill anybody. At least, I hope that isn't the case. We're paying you to keep someone alive. You still interested?"

Clements tossed down the last of his brandy. "Why not? It's the most money anybody ever paid me for keeping someone alive."

Suddenly, the train whistle sounded and the locomotive started to leave the station on its way east. Kell and Joe, who were still standing, took time to steady themselves as the train began to lurch forward. Rachel was already seated.

"This train is headed for Sacramento," Kell explained. "Here at the train depot, there should be a passenger getting on board. There has been a threat against this man's life, should he come westward on the train. It is our job to make sure that nothing happens to him."

"Sounds pretty straight forward to me. Who's the passenger?"

"President Grover Cleveland."

Joe didn't even look surprised by the answer. He had long since quit being surprised by anything Kell did or said. Of all the men Clements had ever known, Kell had more nerve and grit than any of them. Malone was also a man who routinely did the unthinkable. He wasn't afraid of failing in an attempt; he was only afraid of failing to try.

"President Cleveland, huh? Let's hope the killer wants to live more than he wants to assassinate the president."

"What does he mean?" Rachel asked, turning to look at Kell.

"What Joe means," Kell explained, "is that it's nearly impossible to stop a man from killing someone if that man is willing to give his life in the effort."

"Do we know who's behind this plot, Kell?"

"No, we don't."

"Then it could be anyone."

"That's right."

"Kell, does anyone else know your involvement in protecting the president?"

"Only the man who hired us. I don't think anyone else knows."

"But they could?"

"Yes," Kell replied. "And I think I know where you're going with this, Joe."

"Well, *I* don't," Rachel replied. "What are you both talking about?"

Clements looked at Malone for approval. "Should I tell her?"

Kell nodded.

"Your husband and I are thinking the attempt on my life might have something to do with Malone's involvement in this."

"Yeah," Kell said. "If someone knew I would be guarding the president, then it's likely they might also know about my friendship with Joe."

"Oh, I see now," Rachel exclaimed. "They might have thought Joe was coming here to help you." Instantly, the realization came to the woman. She covered her mouth in fear. "Are you saying their attempt on Joe's life might have been to guarantee their success?"

Clements smiled, first at Rachel and then at Malone. "She's a smart one, all right."

"That she is."

"Will you two," Rachel said, "quit talking about me like I'm not even here?"

"Why doesn't the government protect him?" Clements asked.

"That idea's already been talked about, Joe. Some of those in Washington want to form a special government agency, a select group of hand-picked men who do nothing other than protect the president from being assassinated."

"Sounds like a good idea, but what damned fool would want to jump in front of a bullet just to protect a president?"

"You mean like you and Kell just hired on to do?" Rachel asked, with a smug expression.

"Yeah, but this is different, Rachel" Joe explained. "They ain't gonna pay those other damned fools this much money to keep a president alive!"

Chapter Four

As the locomotive approached the Omaha train station, a brass band and a throng of people surrounded President Cleveland. The president was just finishing a rousing speech at the side of the train depot.

Nervously, Jeremiah Langston stood beside him.

"This vigilance on the part of the citizen, and an active interest and participation in political concerns, are the safeguards of his rights," Cleveland stated to the crowd. "But sluggish indifference to political privileges invites the machinations of those who wait to betray the people's trust.

May God bless you all," the president added. "And may God bless the United States of America!"

The crowd erupted into an outpouring of thunderous applause.

Fearing an attempt on the president's life and helpless to do anything but watch, Langston scanned the crowd of well-wishers who eagerly reached out to shake the man's hand.

The former lieutenant had no idea what he might do if someone suddenly produced a gun. For lack of a better idea, Langston silently uttered a prayer.

The short man with the walrus mustache breathed a great sigh of relief as the whistle sounded and the train ground to a halt.

"Finally," he blustered.

Jeremiah saw a familiar face stepping down from the train.

"It's good to see you again, Malone," Langston said, reaching out to shake the hand of the man he formerly commanded in battle. "I wasn't sure you were going to make it."

"Well, I told you I would be here."

"Yes, I know that. However, I just didn't know if it would be today."

"Mr. President! Mr. President!" Langston shouted, raising his voice to be heard above the roar of the crowd. "I want you to meet an old friend of mine. This is Kellen Malone, the man I told you about. He will be accompanying us on our way to Sacramento."

"I am honored to meet you, Mr. Malone." Cleveland said with a smile and a handshake. "I have heard many good things about you."

"The pleasure is all mine, sir. And I would prefer it if you call me Kell." He paused to nod in the direction of Langston. "I would also feel much more comfortable knowing that you chose to believe nothing this man ever says about me."

Cleveland laughed with a deep, rich, and booming voice. "Then, I shall do as you ask. Please call me Grover."

"Enough of this," Kell said, ushering the president inside the train "If I'm to keep you alive, let's get you out of sight."

President Cleveland hesitated briefly. "My wife, Frances, will be joining us, Kell. She is still back at the hotel."

"Okay," Kell said. "Mr. President, I want you to follow me. Langston, you get the woman and bring her here." Malone checked his watch. "And you'd better hurry. The train pulls out in twenty minutes."

***

Leaving her baggage waiting there on the floor, a well-dressed young woman rose from her chair and walked across the lobby to the desk clerk.

"If you would be so kind, sir, could you please tell me what time the train arrives?"

The clerk started to remove his watch from his vest pocket only to be stopped by the sound of a train whistle. "That should be the train coming right now, Mrs. Cleveland."

"Thank you so much."

"I'm just glad to help, ma'am," he said. "Do you need some help with getting your belongings over to the train?"

"No, I don't think so. Thanks. I think someone is coming for me."

"As you wish, ma'am. But please tell me if you change your mind," the clerk said, before returning to his business.

About that moment, a couple of well-armed men in range clothing entered the room. They stood inside the door and briefly surveyed the scene in the lobby. Seeing nobody present but the woman and the desk clerk, the tallest one of the men approached Frances Cleveland.

"Are you the president's wife?" he asked softly, removing his hat as he spoke.

"Yes, I am."

"Pleased to meet you, ma'am. My name is Esau Landry. My brother and I have come to take you to your husband." He nervously peered around the room. "Do you have any luggage to carry?"

"Yes," she replied. "It is right over there."

"Jacob, get the woman's stuff," he ordered, pointing his finger towards the bags. "We need to get going right away."

The brother looked disgusted, but quickly began to gather the woman's things and started walking towards the door.

"But where is Jeremiah?"

"Jeremiah?" Esau asked.

"Yes, Jeremiah Langston, the president's assistant. He told me to wait for him."

"Langston! Yes, that was his name," Landry replied, gently taking her by the arm. "Jeremiah told us to come and get you. The president will be waiting for you, ma'am. We should go now."

"But he said I shouldn't leave until he came back for me."

"Maybe there was a change in plans."

"Not with Jeremiah, there wasn't. The sun doesn't come up in the morning without him scheduling it first."

"I'm sure you're mistaken ma'am," Esau said, taking her by the arm more forcefully this time. "We must go."

"No, I don't think so," Frances blustered, shaking his hand away from her arm. "I'm not going anywhere with you until Jeremiah or my husband returns."

The once gentle eyes of the stranger grew cold and harsh, the glare sending a chill up the woman's spine. Despite his friendly appearance, Esau Landry had killed over a dozen men. His brother, Jacob, had killed almost that many. And he'd savored every one.

"You will be coming with us right now," he said, "if you know what's good for you."

Upon hearing the conversation, the desk clerk left his place behind the counter to see if the president's wife needed his assistance. A veteran of the Indian wars, the desk clerk's gentle tone belied the strength behind this seemingly quiet man.

"I suggest that you leave the woman be," he demanded. His steel-like grip on Esau's shoulder forced the man to turn loose of the woman. "I also suggest you men leave right now."

In his haste to help the woman, the desk clerk had forgotten about the man's brother, who was standing only a few feet behind him. Placing the woman's bags on the floor, Jacob removed his gun, and violently struck the desk clerk in the back of the head with the butt end of his six-gun. The clerk collapsed in a heap on the floor.

For good measure, and for his own twisted entertainment, Jacob slammed a boot toe into the unconscious man's ribcage.

"Now, Mrs. Cleveland," Esau said, motioning towards the door with the barrel of his gun. Jacob's gun was also trained on her. "Let's go."

Before the three of them made it to the door, Langston entered the room.

"Jeremiah!" Frances exclaimed, upon seeing him come through the doorway.

"What's going on here, gentlemen?"

Langston's time in the army had not been wasted. He immediately appraised the situation and knew there was little he could do to prevent the president's wife from being kidnapped. It was obvious that the desk clerk had already been attacked.

"Nothing that concerns you, mister."

"These men are making me go with them, Jeremiah."

"That we are, dude. My brother and I are taking the woman out of here quietly. No harm will come to the president's wife, if she chooses to go along peacefully." Landry and his brother holstered their guns. "And since you were supposed to meet the woman here, you're coming with us to the train. And if you so much as make a peep, we will kill you. Is that understood?"

"I understand." Langston touched Frances on the shoulder to comfort her. "Just do as these men say and it will be all right."

"Come on, Esau," Jacob impatiently grumbled. "Let's get 'em out of here. We've got a train to catch."

"I guess maybe I came at a bad time," said a voice from the doorway. Behind him, a gray, dappled horse nickered softly, just outside at the hitching rail. "And here I was, hoping to get me a room for the night."

The speaker was a tall, older gentleman with white hair and a mustache to match. Framed in the doorway, the old man's lean and wiry figure had an almost angelic appearance, with the rays of sunlight piercing their way around him.

The man spoke quietly, almost apologetically. The only threatening thing about his appearance had to be the gun he wore on his right hip, one that looked like it had seen more than its share of use.

"How long you been standing there?" Esau asked.

"Long enough to know the desk clerk isn't going to be much help to me."

Having murdered several men in his lifetime, Esau wasn't at all intimidated by this man, who was old enough to be his grandfather.

Jacob, the younger of the Landry brothers had never killed a man this old, but he certainly had no qualms about it.

Looking at the two captives, the old man asked, "You folks okay?"

"We're fine," Langston offered.

The former Army lieutenant had never met the man who confronted these outlaws. In fact, he would have bet his last dollar that this kindly, old gentleman was enjoying his last moments of breath on this mortal coil. However, Jeremiah also figured that whatever might happen in the next few minutes might provide enough of a distraction to get the president's wife to safety.

"What about you, ma'am?"

"I'm fine, sir."

Despite her claims to the contrary, there was no missing the fear in the woman's eyes and the quiver in her voice. She was scared. And only a blind man would fail to see it.

"There you have it," Esau said. "You satisfied, now that you know the two of them are finer than frog's hair?"

"Yeah," Jacob added. "Why don't you just be on your way, pappy?"

"My, aren't you an ill-mannered little pup."

"Hey! What do you mean by that?"

"I'll tell you, kid. Back where I come from, your pa would use a willow switch on your backside for talk like that."

"Like to see you try it."

With both of the outlaws focused on the mysterious, old stranger, Langston was ever so slowly ushering the woman towards the hotel desk, safely away from the line of fire. The old man in the doorway immediately recognized Langston's actions for what they were.

"Unfortunately, I don't have a willow switch on me. But I sure wouldn't work up a sweat, turning you over my knee and spanking your backside with your own gunbelt."

Coldly, the young man's eyes glared back at the man. "I think I'm gonna enjoy killing you, old man!"

"That's enough, Jacob," Esau demanded. "Now, mister, do you plan on moving out of the doorway and letting us pass? Or do we have to kill you first," he said, turning his head.

For the first time, Esau noticed that his two captives had inched away from them. As he wheeled around to look, Langston quickly shoved Frances behind the hotel desk.

"Hey! What the....?"

Desperate to stop them from fleeing, Esau went for his gun.

With Esau's attention already directed towards the two captives, the old gunman's hogleg cleared the holster before the older of the Landry brothers ever grabbed iron. The old man's gun stabbed flame and Esau's faded, brown leather vest turned crimson. A second shot from the stranger's six-gun spun the elder Landry around.

The errant shot from the outlaw's gun tore through the wooden hotel desk, just missing the pair who crouched behind it. Then Esau's lifeless body tumbled face-first onto the floor.

As the old man's second shot dispatched the outlaw from this life, Jacob was already firing. His bullet tore a bloody strip along the stranger's left shoulder.

The old gunman winced from the pain, turning his gun on Jacob. He fired once, then twice, both of the bullets leaving their marks, barely inches apart.

Shouting and cursing, Jacob kept firing…

His next two shots sounded as one. The one bullet split the air between the stranger's gun arm and his body. The other slug just missed the old gunman's right ear.

Moving to his left as he fired, the old man emptied his gun into Jacob Landry. The bullets pierced the young outlaw's chest, his body reeling from every successive impact.

Jacob tried to lift his gun, felt his fingers growing numb, and dropped the six-gun at his feet. Bitterly, he cursed the elderly stranger. Then he walked through the open door into the sunlight. He left a bloody trail all the way outside.

Following him out the door, the old gunman quickly punched out the empties and reloaded. Then he holstered his gun.

"Now that there's quite a horse," Jacob exclaimed, while looking at the old man's gray, dappled mount. Finally, Landry's knees buckled and he collapsed in the dusty street, eyes wide open to the sun.

When he came back into the hotel, the stranger kicked away Esau's gun and checked his body for any signs of life. He saw none.

The two captives were rising from their place behind the desk; and he made his way over to them. Jeremiah helped the woman to her feet.

"Are you two okay?" he asked, gently tipping his hat to the lady.

"I am doing quite well," she said, brushing the dust from her clothing, "thanks to you."

"Glad I could help you, ma'am."

"I'm glad too," she said with a smile. "Are they dead?"

"As a hammer, ma'am."

"Thank you, mister," Jeremiah Langston said, extending his hand to the stranger. Gain returned the handshake.

"This, sir, is Frances Cleveland. I am Jeremiah Langston."

"Pleased to meet you both."

"As the man who, in all likelihood, saved our lives, perhaps you would care to share your name with us."

With a bright, friendly smile, the stranger quickly swept the hat from his head and bowed low before them. "You may call me Gain Carson."

"Gain Carson?" he asked with a look of wonder. "Carson...Gain Carson. I know that name! So, you're the man from..."

Gain interrupted the man before he could finish. "Please don't finish that sentence, sir. I know full well who I am."

"I'm sorry."

"It's okay, Mr. Langston. I am often known by a phrase that I don't much care for."

"Well, I will certainly respect your wishes. We both owe you our lives."

"It was my pleasure. Now, before I go, is there anything you need?"

"I am afraid the two of us must hurry and get to the train."

"Pardon me, ma'am. I'm generally a man who believes in minding his own business, but I just have to ask you." He turned his hat over and over in his hands at the same time he rolled a question over in his head. "You wouldn't happen to be the wife of President Cleveland, would you?"

"Yes, I am."

Despite his gratitude for Carson's help, Langston immediately grew suspicious of the old gunman's reason for intervening. With his left arm, he gently nudged Frances behind him for her safety and protection.

"And what is your reason for wanting to know?" Langston asked.

"It matters to me."

"I'm obviously no match for you with a gun, Mr. Carson. But if you intend to harm this woman in any way, I promise I will do my best to stop you."

"I like you, Langston. You've got grit," Carson exclaimed with a gentle smile. "I'm sorry if I've caused you any fear. I mean either of you no harm. In fact, I hope you both will consider me a friend. I am here to make sure that you safely get back to the train. Please follow me."

After this attempt on their lives, Langston still stared at the man with suspicious eyes.

Carson laughed. "If I meant you two any harm, is it likely that I would turn my back on you? Well, that's exactly what I'm planning to do. Now I'm heading for the train. I'll be sure you get there safely, if you care to follow me."

Langston looked at the woman for a sign.

Frances nodded. "We might not be alive if not for his help," she said. "I think we can trust him."

The former Army officer momentarily stopped, quickly debating if he should pick up the dead man's fallen six-gun.

As he reached the doorway, Carson never turned. He never looked behind himself. But he spoke loud enough for the both of them to hear, "Go ahead and pick up that gun, Langston, if you find it gives you a little more security."

Jeremiah stared at the gun like it was a desert rattlesnake. "How did you know I was thinking about it?"

The old gunman continued on his way. "I didn't," he muttered over his shoulder. "Or I didn't until you said so. Now hurry up. We have a train to catch."

***

Nervously, Kell looked at the president and checked his watch. "What's keeping Langston?" he grumbled. "They ought to be back here by now."

"You think something has happened to them?" Cleveland asked.

"I don't know."

Clements spoke up. "Why don't you and Rachel stay here with the president, Malone?' He pulled his six-gun, carefully checked the loads, and then reholstered the gun. "I'll go see what happened to them."

"Well, you be careful, Joe" Rachel said.

"Ain't I always?"

Just then, a knock sounded on the door.

Kell rushed to one side of the door; Clements took the other side. Joe eared back the hammer of his six-gun.

"Who is it?" Malone asked.

"It's Langston, Malone. I've got Frances. Let us in."

"It's about time." Joe grumbled.

Kell quickly opened the door and the two of them bolted into the room.

Clements quickly turned his gun on the old gentlemen who tried to enter the room behind them. "And just who are you, mister?"

"Relax, Joe," Kell said, reaching over with his hand and gently shoving the barrel of Joe's six-gun downward. "He's a friend."

Kell quickly stepped forward and embraced the old man like a long-lost father.

"How are you doing, you old desperado?"

Carson laughed. "Just fine, Kell. You're looking good, boy."

"I hate to be the one to interrupt old home week, but have you forgotten? We've got us a little job to do here," Clements groused. "Why don't we bring this touching reunion inside and close the door behind us?"

"That's right," Kell said. "Come on in."

Carson walked inside, followed by Malone and Clements. Before he shut the door behind them, Joe checked both ways, to see if anyone else was watching them.

"Gain Carson, our nervous friend here is Joe Clements"

"Good to meet you, Joe," Gain said, offering his hand. "I've heard of you."

"I've heard of you, too, mister."

"All good stuff, I hope."

Uncharacteristically, Joe even broke into a smile. "Yep, most of it was."

Gain laughed. Then he made his way over towards the tall, heavy-set gentlemen.

"Gain," Kell replied, "I take it you've already met Langston and Mrs. Cleveland. I want you to meet the President of the United States, Grover Cleveland

"Pleased to meet you, sir," he said, as the two of them shook hands.

"Your two people here," Gain replied, "they ran into a little trouble at the hotel."

"Frances and I might be dead now," Langston blustered, "if Mr. Carson hadn't interceded on our behalf!"

"Then I am forever in your debt, sir" the president said.

"It was my pleasure."

"I know all about you, Mr. Carson. I've read all of the stories by Mr. Haybart."

"With all due respect, Mr. President, then you really don't know all that much about me, not if it came from the pen of Roland Haybart."

"Then you shall have to set me straight, Mr. Carson," he said, with a chuckle. "You *will* be joining us, I take it?"

Gain looked over at Malone, before glancing at Clements.

"Don't look at me," Joe replied. "This here is Malone's tea party. You could say I'm just along for the ride."

Kell nodded.

"I guess I'll be joining you then."

"Splendid!" the president replied. "Perhaps you all will join me for a drink."

"That drink will have to wait, sir," Gain replied. "I have to take care of my horse first."

"You still riding Cochise?" Kell asked.

"Yes, I am."

"I swear, Joe. You should see this horse!" Kell exclaimed. "Finest example of horse flesh I've ever seen."

"That's quite a boast," Joe muttered.

"He's quite a horse," Kell said.

Chapter Five

Ever since President Cleveland boarded the train, Cameron Ellis had been peacefully watching the situation. He certainly was in no hurry. To a man whose profession required him to take the life of others, Cam had learned that the proper moments often presented themselves to the vigilant.

And his patience was always rewarded.

Like a wolf seeking the weakest deer in the herd, Cameron Ellis was content to observe the passengers and his prey. Perhaps a pattern of behavior would develop. Maybe it would eventually reveal a weakness or vulnerability in the president's protective detail.

Those weaknesses or vulnerabilities, Ellis was more than willing to exploit.

He had only to wait.

The wealthy and influential men who hired him were a determined and resourceful lot. They desperately wanted President Cleveland dead. Moreover, they made no provisions for any failure in their mission.

Cam was also aware that his employers might try to hedge their bets, by waging some additional attacks on the president's life. Although he had no way of knowing in what form they might come, he was also aware that the situation might prove to be a useful diversion.

In his attempts to merely blend in with the other passengers, Ellis believed that his study of the situation had gone unnoticed.

Recently, he had started to evaluate the players in this little drama.

Kellen Malone and Joe Clements, Cam knew by name and reputation. Clearly, those two men were capable and tested gunmen, Clements the more reckless of the pair. Ellis was confident that neither of them could match him for speed.

Also joining them in this mission was an older gentleman, with the most remarkable horse that he had ever seen. Ellis hadn't yet been able to come up with a name for the individual, who was undoubtedly no stranger to a six-gun.

As the conductor made his way through the car, Ellis caught his eye.

"May I help you, sir? Mr. Ellis, wasn't it?

"Yes," Ellis replied. "You have an excellent memory. Could you tell me if the train is currently on schedule?"

The conductor removed a watch from his black vest pocket and checked the time. "Yes, we are. In fact, we are a little ahead of schedule."

"That's good to hear."

"You meeting someone?" the conductor asked.

"No," he muttered. "Just have an appointment I have to keep."

At the moment, an attractive woman entered the passenger car on her way back to her room. Several men tipped their hats as she passed. She flashed a brief but grateful smile to each one of them.

Ellis, always being a man who was extraordinarily attracted to the ladies, said nothing as he watched the woman walking through the car. Every swish of her dress drew his attention. Only after the door closed behind her, did the man speak.

"My heavens!" Cam blustered. "Who was that?"

"That is Mrs. Rachel Malone. She is married to Kellen Malone, the tall gentleman who is wearing the twin six-guns."

"Shame to waste a good wedding ring on a gal like that one," he said.

"Now see here, Mr. Ellis. I'll not hear that kind of talk about any lady who is a passenger on this train."

"Please forgive me, sir," Ellis replied, quickly realizing that he wanted to attract no undue interest to his presence. "I certainly meant nothing by the remark."

"Then I apologize, as well," the conductor said. "Perhaps I *was* a bit short with you."

"Your response was understandable."

"Well, I should be on my way now, Mr. Ellis. I hope you enjoy the rest of your trip."

"Thank you kindly. I don't want to keep a busy man from his work. But before you go, maybe you could answer me just one more little question."

"Sure. Go ahead."

"A tall, older gentlemen, wearing a gun, boarded the train a while back."

"Oh, you mean Mr. Carson. Gain Carson." the conductor replied. "The man acquired quite some notoriety in Abilene, Kansas, a while back, as a lawman. If you believe all the stories written about him, he is one of the West's most well-known shootists."

"Do you believe them? The stories, I mean."

"I don't know all that much about gunfighters," the conductor added. "But I can't wait to tell my son I met the legendary Gain Carson. He has read all of Haybart's books, about the man."

"Sounds like we've got several famous people riding this train. Well, I won't take up anymore of your time," Cam said. "You have a good day."

"Same to you, Mr. Ellis."

Swearing underneath his breath, Ellis knew he had been momentarily careless in his remarks about Rachel Malone. Women often made him lose his edge; it was his only weakness. However, Cam believed he had been successful in directing the conductor's attention away from his earlier statement.

Ellis directed his gaze back towards the window, seeing none of the horizon stretched out before him. His fingers lightly tapped the six-gun on his side, concealed behind the tails of his coat. His mind was thinking only of the woman.

***

While looking at the newspaper, the short, balding businessman pushed the eyeglasses back up on his nose. The headline in the paper told everyone that the president was headed westward. As he read the details of the story, he tossed down another drink.

Joseph Blakemore was having second thoughts.

Unlike his fellow conspirators, the wealth he enjoyed hadn't been acquired through violence and bloodshed. Vincent Fielding shared none of those same scruples; the man was an unrepentant killer. Unfortunately, Wilson Stonegate wasn't much better.

Due to his choice of excellent investments and constant diligence in his affairs, Blakemore truly believed that he had earned his station in life. Clearly, he had no desire to lose those things for which he devoted a lifetime of labor.

A knock sounded on the door of his elaborate Sacramento office.

"Come on in," Blakemore said. "The door's open."

"Joseph," Stonegate said, "I'm glad to finally catch up with you."

"What do you want, Wilson?"

"I was starting to think you were trying to avoid me."

"And why would I do that?"

"You tell me, Joseph. You've been unusually quiet since we made our deal with Fielding."

"You mean our deal with the devil?"

"Now what kind of talk is that?"

Blakemore rose from his chair, poured himself a drink, and poured another one for Stonegate. He handed it to the man.

"Thanks, Joseph," Wilson replied, clinking his glass against that of his friend. "Cheers."

"Cheers," Blakemore said.

The two men tossed back their drinks.

"You call it a deal; I call it murder."

"Of course it's murder," Wilson blustered. "But that doesn't mean it isn't necessary. If Cleveland continues to pursue these policies, then we will be ruined. I'm just not willing to let that happen. Are you?"

"I know. I know. It just seems to me that there has to be some alternative, some other way to do this."

"There isn't any other way, Joseph. Since we cannot go back and change the results of the election, this is our only viable option."

Despite Stonegate's appeals to the contrary, Blakemore didn't appear to be convinced. Still holding the empty liquor glass, he paced the floor from one side of the office to the other. Finally, his heavy body plumped back down in his chair.

"Well, don't you be getting cold feet on us, Joseph!"

"I'm not getting cold feet."

"Are you sure? That isn't what it looks like to me." Stonegate said, the tone of his voice growing higher as he became agitated or concerned. "And I don't need to tell you what Vincent might do, if he thinks you're planning on getting out."

"Don't worry about me, Wilson. I'm a little scared, not foolish."

"Good," he said. "I'm glad to hear you say that. You and I both know that Vincent Fielding is not the kind of man you want to cross."

"Now, Wilson," Blakemore said, momentarily setting his concerns aside, "what did you want to speak to me about?"

Stonegate smiled to himself, as he rose to pour himself another drink. "Want one?"

"No," Joseph said. "Had enough already."

"Suit yourself," he replied, tossing down the second drink. "I know you're nervous about this thing. So am I. In fact, I am not all that confident that, good as he's reported to be, Cameron Ellis is any match for Kellen Malone."

"Kellen Malone?"

"Yes," Stonegate said. "Malone! You mean you didn't know the former Army hero is the man protecting the president?"

"No, I didn't. It sounds like maybe I should have joined you in that drink, after all."

"Well, I just learned about it the other day, Joseph. Didn't much care for the odds," he said, with a confident smile. "As a man who loves a good game of poker, I thought it was time we stacked the deck a little more in our favor."

"What do you mean?"

"I hired a man that worked for me before. He's getting a team together. They are going to attack the president's train."

"Do you think it will work?"

"Like I said, I like the odds a lot better than just counting on Cam Ellis."

"Sounds kind of risky."

"Not as risky as a noose."

"Can't argue with you there. Does Vincent know?"

"No."

"What will he think," Joseph said, "if he learns you went behind his back?"

"Fielding doesn't care about anything other than seeing Cleveland dead. I doubt that the means of his execution will make any difference to the man."

In spite of his fears, Blakemore suddenly broke into laughter at Stonegate's strange choice of words.

"What's so funny?"

"I wish you wouldn't use the term *execution*."

"For men conspiring to assassinate a president," he said with a smile, "perhaps I should have used another term." Then his features turned sober. "Trust me, Joseph. Everything should go according to plan. And if my man fails, there is still Cameron Ellis."

As much as he deplored violence, Blakemore decided that he feared poverty more. Moreover, the die had already been cast on their plans. There could be no turning back now.

"One thing you are forgetting, Wilson."

"What's that?"

"There is still Kellen Malone."

Chapter Six

In his desire to protect his boss, Jeremiah Langston had insisted that the president have one car, with a couple of elaborate rooms reserved only for Grover and Frances Cleveland. This car was towards the rear of the train, one car away from the caboose.

Other than the conductor, nobody ever entered this car without the full knowledge and permission of Malone or Langston, only.

Once, a couple of curiosity seekers had sought to make their way back to speak to their esteemed fellow traveler, President Cleveland. However, upon trying to enter the president car, the naïve pair of well-wishers were quickly greeted with a host of hard stares and cold steel.

In between the president's car and the caboose, was the car shared by his troops and bodyguards. Kellen Malone and Rachel had one of those rooms to themselves, although much of their trip was spent accompanying the president and his wife. In general, Cleveland was guarded by individual shifts, which were split between Kell, Joe Clements, and Gain Carson.

In a few rare instances, a situation would occur that would require two or three of them to be there at the same time.

After the unfortunate incident with the unexpected visitors, the president, not wanting to seem aloof to his constituents, insisted that he make an occasional rare visit to the forward cars of the train. With the threats that had already been directed towards his life, these visits were sources of great consternation for all those entrusted with protecting the man's life.

While Kell, Joe and Gain were off on one the presidential forays with the common folk, a gentle knock sounded on the door of Malone's room.

Rachel, looking radiant after just having freshened up a little, was smiling when she opened her door to the blue-coated trooper, a soldier who was hand-picked by Malone, and appointed by the president, for this specific mission.

"Good evening, Dent," she said.

Quickly removing his hat, Captain Denton Turner blushed slightly, momentarily forgetting what he had to say, as he always did in the presence of an attractive woman.

"Good evening to you, ma'am."

"I wish you would call me Rachel. We've known each other long enough for that."

"I can't do that, ma'am," he replied, fumbling to hold onto his hat.

"Sure you can. And I am sure Kell wouldn't mind. After all, we've known each other since you protected me back in Arizona."

"But that was my job, ma'am."

"No, it wasn't. As I recall, you spoke of arresting Kell at the time."

Nervously, Turner looked both ways, to assure that nobody heard her statement. "If it's all the same to you, ma'am, I would prefer to forget the context of those unfortunate events. Your husband—not that he was your husband then—broke the law."

"I know, Dent. But it was still awfully sweet of you."

Turner's mind went suddenly blank.

Although he welcomed this hazardous duty, to which he'd been personally assigned by the president, Turner suddenly wished to be elsewhere. Women continually made him uncomfortable. But it was never more so, than at this moment.

The woman stood there, staring at him, saying nothing.

Drops of sweat began to break out on his forehead.

"You knocked on my door, Dent. Did you need something?"

"Oh, yes," he said, his face turning a dozen shades of red. "Sorry to trouble you, Mrs. Malone, but I have a letter addressed to you."

"Thank you, Dent," she replied with a smile.

Not only did the woman smell nice, her constant need to smile was enough to leave him longing for those tense hours of facing Apache hostiles, in the brutal Arizona desert.

"You're welcome, ma'am," he muttered, fighting his sudden compulsion to stutter.

He breathed a sigh of relief when Rachel closed the door behind her.

Rachel looked at the letter before opening it. Her name was written on the front; there was nothing to identify the sender.

She tore the note open and began to read the contents. Immediately, she broke into tears and threw open the door.

"Captain!" she exclaimed. "Captain!"

Gun drawn, Turner came charging towards her door. Expecting danger, he scanned the hallway and her quarters for any threats.

"What is it, ma'am?"

"I need you to get, Kell. Right now."

"Yes, ma'am."

Turner motioned to one of the more junior soldiers, "You stay here next to the door until I return. You understand? Nobody—and I mean nobody—but Malone is to come anywhere close to this room until I return."

"Understood, sir," the young man said.

Kell returned a few minutes later with Captain Turner. The young trooper stepped aside so Malone and Turner could enter the room.

"What is it, Rachel?"

She threw herself into his arms while still holding the letter, the paper still wet from her tears. Seeing that she was clearly frightened, Kell firmly returned her embrace.

"I'm glad you're here," she said, handing him the note. "Look!"

Kell quickly scanned the contents of this letter. His brow furrowed. "Where did you get this?"

"Captain Turner gave it to me."

Malone directed his gaze towards Turner. "What about it, Dent?"

"I really don't know what to tell you, sir. The conductor gave me the note. Told me to deliver it to Mrs. Malone."

"Who gave it to him?"

"He didn't know where it came from. Said he found it in the hallway of one of the forward cars. Figured it belonged to your missus." Quizzically, Turner looked at Malone. "What is it, sir?"

"The note told Rachel that I will never leave the train alive if the president reaches Sacramento in one piece. It also said a couple of other things about Rachel that I wouldn't much care to repeat."

"Do you believe it's real."

Kell nodded. "I believe it's a real threat."

Thinking out loud, Captain Turner said the words that everybody else was already thinking.

"Sounds like somebody on this train may be a killer."

"Or something worse," Kell added.

***

Clements was strangely silent after he read the note that Rachel received. He refolded the letter and handed it back to Malone. Malone said nothing as he waited for Joe to build a smoke.

Clements took out his makings, held them for a moment, and then returned them to his pocket. The scar-faced gunman leaned back against the door of the railroad car, coolly staring off into space.

"So, what do you think, Joe?"

"I think we have a lot more to worry about, Malone, than just the life of the president."

"That's the same conclusion I reached."

Using his thumb to point at the car behind his back, Clements said, "Did you notice the man on the right side, by himself. Something about that guy is familiar to me."

"Yeah, Joe. I saw him too. Looks like a hard case. It also seems like he spends a lot of effort looking disinterested."

"You caught that too?"

"Yeah, I did."

"What do you want to do about him?" Joe said. "He doesn't look to be wearing a gun; but I'd bet my last dollar he has one on."

"Let's just keep our eye on the man for now."

"You got it." This time, Clements actually rolled himself a cigarette. After lighting it, he looked at Malone. "Had a man offer me a job the other day. Good money, too!"

"What else is new?"

"This job kind of appealed to me, Malone. Kind of hard to turn it down. Figured it would be easy money."

"Why'd you pass it up?"

"Darned if I know."

"Never knew you to turn down a job for top dollar. What made you let it go?"

"Two reasons."

"And those were?"

"The first was a good looking redhead, named Jenny."

"Sounds like a good reason to me," Kell said with a smile. "What about the second?"

"I kind of figured life might get kind of boring without him around." He exhaled a long trail of smoke. Then Clements smiled. "Mostly, I was scared of his wife. Rachel has grown kind of attached to the guy."

"Sounds like this hombre," Kell replied, "might be a little tough to kill."

"Would be for most people—not me. I've seen a couple of times I might have done it for two bits."

Malone laughed. "A couple of times, Rachel might have given you the two bits."

Laughing at the remark, Clements flicked away his cigarette.

"Are you saying you passed on the job?"

"Not sure yet," Joe replied. "Still giving it some thought. Got to see if Rachel will match the offer."

"Well, let me know what the two of you decide."

"Starting to have second thoughts," he said. "It *was* a lot of money."

"Maybe next time."

"I don't think there will be a next time," Joe said. "We didn't part on the best of terms. But Jenny and I definitely had a meeting of the minds."

Joe looked at the rumpled paper that Kell was still holding in his hands.

"You need to get rid of that letter, Malone. Tear it up; throw it away. Just somebody trying to scare you, take away your edge. We ain't gonna let nothing happen to Rachel."

"Thanks, Joe."

"I don't care about anyone threatening our lives, Malone. We're used to that." His green eyes turned cold. "I'll flat out kill the man who puts a finger on Rachel."

"You'll have to wait in line behind me."

"That's fine, too. I'll kill whatever's left of him, after you're done."

***

While Malone and Clements were making their rounds, the president and Gain Carson took a few moments to share some cigars and brandy.

"So, Mr. Carson," the president said, testing his drink.

"Please call me Gain."

"As you wish, Gain. I would personally be grateful if you would call me Grover."

"Please excuse me, sir, but you're the president. To me, that seems a little disrespectful of your high office."

"We're alone now. And it isn't out of line," Cleveland said, taking a long pull from his cigar, "not for a couple of old lawmen like us."

"You were a lawman?"

"Yes, I was. I was Sheriff of Erie County, New York."

Gain smiled. "Then Grover it is."

"Excellent," the president replied. "However, I'm sure my time as a sheriff wasn't nearly as exciting or as noteworthy as your time in Abilene, Gain."

"Hogwash!"

The president laughed out loud. "I just love you Westerners! For a man whose position often requires people catering to his every whim, it's refreshing to meet someone who doesn't join them.

"I would rather the man who presents something for my consideration subject me to a zephyr of truth and a gentle breeze of responsibility rather than blow me down with a curtain of hot wind. Now," Cleveland said, "please tell me what you meant by your last statement."

Carson downed the last of his drink. "It means that any lawman who faithfully executes his duty is worthy of the public's respect."

"That's kind of you to say."

"It isn't just kind, Grover; it's true."

"By the way, Gain, how did you happen to be in town when the bandits tried to kidnap my wife?"

Gain took a pull from his cigar before answering. "Kell sent me a telegraph, asking for my help. Said I was to meet him here. The rest of it? That was simply pure, dumb luck."

"Sounds like you are a master of good timing."

At that moment, the door burst open. Gain's hand flashed for his gun.

"Relax, old friend," Kell replied. "It's just us."

"If he shoots us, Malone," Clements replied, "I'm never going to let you forget it."

"If he shoots us, Joe, neither will I."

"Your wife is in the next car with Mrs. Malone, Langston, and a couple of the soldiers," Malone said to Cleveland. "She should be safe in there. And Langston knows how to use that scattergun."

"You're just in time, gentlemen," the president said, "to join us for a drink and a cigar."

"I think I'll pass on that drink," Malone stated, "but the cigar sounds mighty tempting."

Clements plopped down into a chair and said, "Kell's like an old school marm," he muttered, "always trying to behave himself while on the job."

"The cigars and brandy are gonna to have to wait," Kell said, while looking out the window. "We have riders headed this way."

Clements didn't even wait for instructions. He drew his gun, threw open the door, and raced for the back of the train.

Kell paused briefly in the door. "You stay with the president, Gain. If anyone comes in this door without identifying himself, it's your job to stop them."

"You can count on me, Kell," Gain replied.

"Never doubted it for a moment, Gain. Keep your head down, Mr. President. One more thing," Kell added. "You need to listen close. If Gain can't stop them, use that six-gun I stashed underneath the sofa cushion.

"These are unsavory men, sir. They've already tried to kidnap your wife to achieve their purposes," Malone explained. "Don't bother shooting unless you plan to kill them."

"Understood!"

Kell closed the door behind him. He sprinted to the door between the cars, opened it, and looked both ways for the riders. Seeing none of the outlaws alongside of them, Kell scrambled up the ladder to the top of the railroad car.

From his high position, Kell could count no fewer than eight horses and riders. He guessed that some may have already climbed aboard the train.

The shooting had already started.

Chapter Seven

Approximately a dozen armed men were approaching the train when Clements reached the caboose. A couple of the outlaws had leaped from their horses and were already aboard the train. Others were attempting to reach the caboose.

Several of the union soldiers, accompanying the president, were firing at the riders. At least three of them already lay dead or dying.

Joe triggered his six-gun as fast as he could fire, sending a pair of the riders backwards over their saddles. When his gun went empty, he holstered it, picking up one of the rifles from a dead soldier.

Taking careful aim at another of the horsemen, Clements coolly squeezed off a shot, killing another one of the riders. He winced in pain as a bullet creased the fleshy part of his arm.

Joe turned to face the shooter, who was now aboard the train.

The man missed his second shot at Clements. He wouldn't get a third.

Joe clubbed him with the barrel of the rifle, knocking him to the floor. He took aim at the fallen man, but the gun was now empty.

The outlaw, strangely agile for a big man, scrambled to his feet with a knife.

"You shouldn't have let me get up, mister."

"I won't make that mistake again. Spending too much of my time lately, keeping company with school marms."

The man grinned wickedly. "Too bad for you; you won't get another chance."

"You gonna use that knife or just bore me all day talking about it?"

Joe, holding nothing but an empty rifle, waited on the man's attack. His cool, green eyes showed no fear or reservation.

The outlaw charged at him with the knife, scarcely missing Clements' ribs.

Joe wheeled around with the rifle, the blow sending the outlaw over the railing. Desperate to live and to kill, the man clung to the railing.

Clements had already touched the sandy bottom in his well of mercy.

Cruelly, his rifle butt crushed the man's skull and loosed him from the railing. The outlaw's bloody and lifeless form tumbled over and over on the railroad tracks.

After slowing the initial brunt of the attack, Joe was joined at the back of the train by several more of the blue-coated troopers. They boldly carried the fight to the remaining enemies.

Gunfire, coming from the top of the train, indicated that several of the assassins had gotten by him. Thumbing cartridges into his empty six-gun, Joe headed for the president's railroad car.

***

As Malone's head cleared the top of the railroad car, he felt the deadly whiff of a bullet next to his jaw.

Kell snapped off a shot and left a growing crimson stain on the chest of the approaching gunman, whose body then tumbled from the roof of the car. Before Malone could take another shot, the second man knocked him down with a rolling body block.

Viciously, the man tried to stomp the life out of him with his boot.

Malone evaded the man's boot, but not the spur. The jagged metal rowel cut him to the skin, leaving a bloody stripe across his vest.

Desperate to finish Malone off, the outlaw's gun quickly cleared leather.

Malone scrambled for his fallen gun. He dived to pick it up, rolling over on his back to draw. The movement caused the outlaw to miss.

Malone's gun came up and fired twice, hitting the man in the throat and also cutting the tobacco sack he carried in his shirt pocket.

The man was game, his increasingly numb fingers trying to trigger the gun. He advanced on Malone, staggered suddenly, and his lifeless body tumbled on top of Kell.

Malone pushed the bloody man's body off of him, just in time to see another outlaw jumping from the next car to his.

Malone's gun flamed again, a second shot coming from behind him.

The two shots sounded as one, both slugs sending the fallen outlaw's body down between the two cars.

Malone rolled over, leveling the gun on the shooter behind him.

He relaxed when he saw the smiling scarred face of Joe Clements.

"That was some fine shooting there, Malone," Clements said with a smile. "Second best man I ever knew with a gun. If you're done playing, maybe we should check on the president."

Malone came to his feet in time to see a man training his rifle on Joe. His six-gun bucked in his hand, sending the riderless horse racing away, with stirrups wildly slapping his sides.

"I guess I owe you one, Malone."

"You owe me several, Joe. Now let's go check on the president."

As they made their way to the president's car, Malone and Clements found themselves staring into the barrels of the troopers' guns.

"It's okay," Gain said, the men relaxing their aim only after Carson spoke.

Joe and Kell had to step over a couple of dead bodies just outside the doorway to the president's car. Gain stood silently, punching out the empty cartridges and replacing them with fresh ones.

"Is everyone okay here?" Kell asked.

"Thanks to Gain," the president stated, "we are none the worse for wear. Will you please check on Frances, Mr. Malone? There was gunfire next door."

"Yes, I will, sir." Kell motioned at Joe. "You stay here with him. I'll check on the ladies."

Clements nodded.

Kell quickly moved to Rachel's room, seeing the assassin's nearly-disemboweled remains, the remnants of a nearby shotgun blast.

More armed, blue-coated troopers surrounded the door. Kell looked inside, seeing the president's wife, Langston, and Rachel were unharmed.

Scared for his safety during the attack, Rachel ran to her husband, throwing her arms around the man.

"You're bleeding, Kell!"

"No, I'm not. It's somebody else's."

"You sure?"

Kell laughed. "I'm sure, Rachel. Being shot is generally not something I'm uncertain about."

Rachel slapped him on the arm. Then she stood on her tip toes to softly kiss him on the lips. He returned her embrace. "I'm glad you're okay, Kell."

"Me, too. Is everybody all right here?"

"Yes," Langston said. "One of them tried to force his way inside."

"May I go see the president?" Frances asked.

"Sure you can. I think it's safe now." Kell nodded at Captain Turner. "Don't let her out of your sight, Dent! Not unless Joe Clements is with them."

"Understood, sir," the man replied, snapping off a quick salute.

"Let's go, ma'am," he said to Mrs. Cleveland.

Kell said nothing further, until the president's wife had left the room.

"Well, looks like the old lieutenant remembered what to do with a scattergun."

"It's a good thing he did," Rachel stated.

Now that the excitement had died down, and the gunfire subsided, Langston sunk down into a chair. With a somewhat greenish appearance to this face, the former Army officer dropped the empty double barrel to the floor.

"Are you okay, Langston? Please get this man a drink, Rachel."

Rachel moved to the counter, found a glass, and poured the man a shot of brandy. She handed it to her squeamish-looking guardian, and he drank it down in one swallow.

"Did that help any?" Malone asked.

"Not much," he muttered, handing Rachel the glass. "Could you pour me another?"

He nodded as he took the second drink from the woman and tossed it down as well.

"I guess I forgot what it felt like to kill a man. How do you ever get used to it?"

"You don't," Kell replied. "You just learn to live with it."

"That isn't much comfort."

"No, it isn't" Kell added. "It isn't much comfort at all."

Now that the fighting was all over, Kell needed to get outside. He picked up a cigar from the desk and started outside. He patted Rachel on the arm, "Tell Joe that I went outside to get me some air."

"Okay, Kell. Please be careful."

He laughed. "I think the worst of it is over, for now. I'll be right back."

Malone carefully closed the door behind him.

"You men," he said, nodding at the soldiers, "until I return, make sure nobody goes into these rooms other than Joe Clements or Gain Carson. Is that understood?"

They all nodded. And knowing the man's decorated history with the Army, a couple of them saluted.

Malone made his way out onto the deck between the trains. The pungent smell of gunsmoke still lingered in the air. Striking a match on the rail, he lit the cigar and took a couple of deep puffs. He looked out toward the horizon, feeling the rumbling of the train as it moved on its journey westward.

Before Malone finished his cigar, the door opened from one of the other cars. The lean, wolfish-looking man who joined him there was the man they saw in the train.

"Howdy, stranger," the man said, quickly building a smoke.

Kell nodded, exhaling the smoke from his puff on the cigar. Seeing the man was almost done with his makings, Kell reached into his vest pocket, removing another match. He struck it on the rail. "Please allow me."

The stranger leaned closer to Kell's cupped hand.

"Thanks, friend," the man added, taking a pull from his cigarette. "It was quite some excitement we had there. My name's Cam."

"Pleased to meet you, Cam. They call me Kell, Kellen Malone."

"I've heard of you. Is the president okay?"

"Yes, he is."

"Well, that's good. Nobody wants another Ford's Theater, taking place on this train."

"No, they don't." Kell stared the man in the face. "If you don't mind me asking, where are you headed?

"No, I don't mind you asking at all," he replied, feigning a smile. "Nowhere special, I guess. I thought I might check out some business interests in Sacramento. The other passengers feel a lot better, being on a train with men like you guarding the president."

Kell stubbed the end of his cigar on the railing, tossed it aside, and turned his back to the man. He leaned his elbows on the rail and watched a herd of cattle grazing in a rich, green meadow. "This is beautiful country, don't you think?"

"Yes, it is."

"You know, Cam. I always do my best thinking outside. And something just struck me as kind of odd," he said, speaking over his shoulder to the man behind him. "I just keep running it over and over again in my mind. What makes you think it wasn't just a simple train robbery?"

"Thinking too much is a good way to get yourself killed," Cam said, flicking away the cigarette. He drew his six-gun to emphasize the point. "And don't even think of going for those guns. You'll be dead before you even clear leather."

"I also wondered how you knew I was guarding the president." Kell turned around to face a gun directed at his belly. "Nobody except the conductor knew that information."

"The bad thing about secrets, Cameron said with a chuckle, "is that everybody who has one wants to let people know they have one."

"Ain't it just terrible?" Kell muttered, shaking his head. "Why didn't you make your play during the attack."

"Come on now, Mr. Malone. A thinking man like you knows the answer to that one. Hell, I even figured it might work. Didn't really matter much to me, either way. Figured you would all let your guard down after you stopped them. And here we are."

"How do you plan on playing this?"

"We're going to walk quietly," the gunman said, "like two old friends to the president's car. Then you are going to introduce me to the man. It doesn't even have to go bad for you, Malone. I just want the president."

"That isn't going to happen, Cam. You *are* Cameron Ellis, I take it?"

"Well, you are a thinking man, after all, Malone," he observed with a cruel smile. "Well done, but some of your thinking's a little flawed. You're holding no high cards in this hand. Now take me to the president!"

"Nope. Guess you're just going to have to kill me."

"You know full well I can't pull this trigger, Malone. One shot and those troopers will come running like bees to honey."

Just then, the conductor came out the door behind Ellis. Failing to see the gun pointed at Malone's gut, he said, "I just wanted to see if you required anything, Mr. Malone."

Moving swiftly, Cam grabbed the man by the arm, pulling the conductor in front of him for cover. He pointed his gun at the back of the man's neck.

Malone's guns already sprung to his hands.

"Now, Mr. Malone, you know I'll kill this man. Now holster those guns! It's time we go see the president."

Malone nodded, returning his guns to their holsters.

"Now, you are going to lead the way, Mr. Thinking Man. If I see anything I don't like, then this man's blood will be on your hands. You understand that, Malone?"

"Yes, I do."

Suddenly, Kellen Malone broke into a wide smile.

"I'm the one holding the gun, Malone. What are you grinning about?"

"The man standing behind you."

Cam laughed. "You don't think I'm foolish enough to fall for that old trick, do you, Malone?"

Kell shook his head. "Probably not. But it was worth a try."

"Enough of these games," Cam said. "Now let's move!"

Just then, Joe Clements put a six-gun's muzzle to the back of Cam's skull and gently eared back the trigger. When Cam released his grip on the man, the conductor eagerly stepped out of the line of fire.

"Now, Cam, this thinking man is thinking you ought to hand that gun over to me," Kell said. "Don't you think so, Cam? How about you, Joe? What do you think?"

"I'm thinking it sounds like some sage advice to me," Clements muttered. "I think you would be wise to follow it."

Ellis flipped his gun over to Malone, who caught it with one hand. Without saying another word, Kell walked up to the gunman.

"Now, why don't you tell us who hired you? We know you don't do anything without being paid."

"My clients expect a little discretion," Cameron said, his eyes holding nothing but contempt for Malone.

"He won't tell you anything, Malone," Joe added. "You're wasting your time."

"I'm thinking that's too bad for him," Kell stated. "Might have spared him a rope."

Ellis gave them both a smug and triumphant smile. "Please be sure and give my regards to the lovely Mrs. Malone."

Kell said nothing as he advanced towards the man, fiercely striking him across the skull with the pistol butt.

Malone caught the man's unconscious body before it fell down on the deck between the cars. He handed Cam's gun to Clements. Then taking Ellis by the shirt and the back of the belt, Kell flung the man's body off the side of the train.

The man's body bounded over the hill like a rag doll down a cliff side.

Clements, who rarely saw anything in this life that ever surprised him, was startled by Kell's uncharacteristically-violent action.

The conductor gasped in horror. "What kind of man throws an unconscious passenger off a train?"

"A man," Kell blustered, "who is tired of having guns pointed at us."

"You should have killed him, Malone," Joe said.

"What makes you so sure that he hasn't?" the conductor said. "Even if the man survives the fall, he's out there in the wilderness with no water and no horse. Some folks would call that a death sentence."

"He should have thought of that before he pulled a gun on me."

"Pure evil like that don't die with anything less than a bullet," Joe observed, turning his gaze back to Malone. "You know he will be back for you, don't you?'

"Yeah, I know."

"The next time, just make sure you put him down for good."

"You can count on it."

Clements pulled his hat down a little lower over his eyes and turned to go back inside. He paused at the door.

"Someone tossing a gunman like Cameron Ellis off a moving train," he said with a smile, "now that's a sight I never thought I would see. I do have to like your style, Malone. Starting to think you're meaner than me."

"Now that's a frightening thought."

"Probably not a good idea," Joe observed, "for him to say anything about Rachel."

"Probably not," Kell said.

Chapter Eight

"How many good men died in protecting my life?" the president said.

"Two, sir," Captain Turner replied.

"That is truly a shame," he said. "I would like to send a personal letter, expressing my sorrow over their sacrifices, to each of their wives and families. Will you see about getting their names and addresses for me, Captain?"

"Yes, sir," Turner said. "You can count on it."

"Thank you, Captain," the president said, reaching out and placing a firm hand on his shoulder. "And one other thing."

Suddenly, Denton Turner realized that he was nearly as nervous, as when he was speaking to Malone's wife. He quickly struggled to regain his military bearing.

"What is that, sir?"

"I want to thank you, young man, for your courage. Please be sure and pass along my appreciation to every man in your detail. Will you do that for me?"

"Yes, sir. We're just honored to serve you."

"And I am truly honored by your service."

Like the devoted military veteran that he certainly was, Turner gave President Cleveland his finest military salute, turned on his heels, and went off to carry out the orders of his Commander-in-Chief.

When the president turned back around to face the others gathered in the room, he was visibly shaken.

"I am not sure if any nation's chief executive is worthy of this level of bloodshed," he stated. "Please allow me to express my appreciation for the risks that all of those in this room have taken on my behalf. I will forever remain in your debt."

While nobody in the room spoke, Frances embraced the president. The silence was finally broken by Joe Clements.

He slapped his hand on his leg. "Now I know where I saw Ellis!"

"What are you talking about, Joe?" Kell said.

"Cam Ellis, the guy you threw off the train."

"You threw a man off the train?" Langston blustered.

Malone motioned for Langston to be silent. "What about Ellis?"

"I finally remembered where I had seen Ellis before. It was in Denver, when the man tried to hire me to kill you."

Now it was Rachel's turn to interrupt the conversation. "What do you mean, Joe?" she said, with a look of astonishment. "Did someone really try to give you money to murder my husband?"

"Yes," Joe said.

"Did you take it?" she asked, looking him directly in the face.

"Just for a moment," he said with a laugh. "It did pain me to give it back."

"That's not funny, Joe!" she said.

"Yeah, it kinda was," Malone replied.

"And that will be enough out of you, Kellen Malone! This isn't funny at all. I'm your wife. You should have told me about this."

"It isn't like I had a lot of time," Malone said, gently patting her on the arm. "Now, Joe, if you can get back to your story."

"When I was in Denver, Fielding gave me an envelope filled with cash."

Langston cut him off before he could say anything more.

"Fielding, you say. Was that Vincent Fielding?"

"Yes, it was," Joe said.

"Mr. President," Langston said, "Vincent Fielding is one of your most vocal critics, involving your decision to return those vast tracts of acreage to the public domain."

"Jeremiah," the president scolded, "please let the man finish."

"But, Mr. President," Langston pleaded, "it's not unreasonable to assume that Fielding might have some part in this conspiracy."

"Just because he wanted Malone dead?" Clements said. "Lots of people like that."

Still angry over this newest revelation, Rachel's arms were folded and she continued to glare at Clements. His latest remark only served to stoke the flames.

Malone winked at Clements.

"What about this Mr. Ellis?" Frances said, no longer able to contain her curiosity.

"Anyway, after I turned the job down," Clements replied, with a nod towards Rachel, "Fielding stormed out of the saloon. Ellis was there, too. He left not long after Fielding did."

"So, do you think there was some connection between the two men?" Langston said.

"Yes," Joe replied, "I do."

"Why'd you throw him off the train?" Rachel asked.

"Because I think he was the one who wrote the letter," Malone replied.

"What letter?" Langston said.

"The letter that threatened my life if the president lived," Malone said, "and made some vile references to Rachel."

"I didn't know anything about a threatening letter," Frances said, looking at the president.

"Me, either," Langston added.

Cleveland shrugged. "This is the first I've heard about it, too."

All eyes were suddenly directed at Kellen Malone.

"Now I'm starting to remember," Joe mumbled softly, "why I never discuss my business in public."

"Then why did you decide throw Ellis off the train?" Langston said. "We might have questioned him."

"I did question him," Malone said. "He wouldn't talk."

"How hard did you try?" Langston asked.

"He's right, Langston," Joe added. "Men like Ellis will die before they'll talk. But when he said something about Rachel, Kell knocked him out with his gun and tossed him over the rail."

"This is just like the war," Langston replied, still fuming about Kell's actions. "You shouldn't have made that decision without discussing it with me first."

"It wasn't a decision," Kell explained. "And this isn't Antietam. But I'm not letting anybody talk that way about my wife."

"Thank you, Kell," Rachel said.

"Listen, Langston," Joe said, his cool green eyes locked on the former Army officer, "if you're not satisfied with the job we are doing, I would be more than happy to fork a horse for Denver. Maybe then, you can get somebody else to protect the president!"

With a wry smile on his face, Gain Carson was sitting off to one side, quietly listening to the increasingly heated exchange. Suddenly, he leaned over and patted the president on the arm. "This conversation," Gain said, "is some of the most fun I've had in quite some time."

President Cleveland laughed out loud at his remark.

"Does Mr. Clements speak for you, Kell?" Langston said.

"No, he doesn't. Joe is here because I asked him, Langston. I signed on with you to protect the president, and I'll see it to the end," Malone said, strongly. "The president is alive right now, because Joe and I know what we're doing. Let's be clear about a couple of things, Langston. I want Joe here. And you don't get any say so about my methods. Is that understood?"

Langston started to reply, but was cut short by the president.

"Gentlemen! Gentlemen!" the president shouted.

The room grew quiet, the silence broken only by Carson's laughter.

"Despite our current behavior, the enemy is outside these doors," the president said. "We shouldn't be fighting amongst ourselves. And, Jeremiah, I have every confidence in these men. Moreover, I have every confidence in you! You made a wise selection in your choice.

"Kellen Malone and Joe Clements are a couple of hard and dangerous men. I've read their files; I've shaken their hands. I've looked deep into their eyes. Clearly, they are not the sort of men you want to have as enemies. But I do believe," Cleveland added, "that any individual would truly be fortunate and blessed to have men, such as these, standing there beside him. Thank you, gentlemen."

Smiling brightly, Frances gently touched the president's arm. She took a moment to look each one of her protectors in the eye. "You have my gratitude, as well."

Playfully, Gain swatted the president on the back. "Good!" he said. "I guess this calls for a round of drinks."

"And some fine cigars," Cleveland added.

***

The welcome morning smells of hot coffee and sizzling bacon drove the sore and weary stranger towards the campfire.

His clothes were torn, stained, and dirty. There were scratches and some minor cuts, several places on his body. Upon regaining consciousness, he was pleased to realize that none of his bones were broken. He knew it could have been much worse.

The very first rays of sunlight were just breaking upon the horizon.

"Hail the camp," he shouted. "Mind if I come in?"

"Come on ahead. And come in slow and careful," the man said, covering the stranger with his gun as he approached. "I'll turn no man away from my fire."

Upon seeing the stranger was unarmed, as he walked into the light from the flames, the man holstered his gun.

"Go ahead," he said, nodding towards the fire. "You look about done in. And I've about had my fill."

Hungrily, the man helped himself to bacon and a cold biscuit. He began wolfing down the food, as his benefactor handed him a cup of hot coffee. The man giving him the cup was wearing a badge.

"Thank you, friend," he said, momentarily looking up from his food.

"Good to meet you. My name's Frye. Deputy Aiden Frye."

"My name's Cal Evans."

"What happened to you, Cal?"

"Outlaws," he said. "Beat me, took my gun, my gear, and my horse. Left me for dead."

"How many were there?"

"There were three of them, Deputy."

"Well, they must not be headed west," Frye said. "That's the direction I was coming from. And I never cut their trails."

"Probably a good thing you didn't run into them," Cal said. "They were bad men."

Frye laughed. "I've had some experience with bad men."

Evans poured himself a second cup of coffee. Then he stirred at the fire with a broken branding rod that Frye was using for a poker. He added another log to the blaze.

"I'm headed east of here," the Deputy said. "Don't have an extra horse. But you're welcomed to double up until we get to town."

"Thanks, Deputy. I may just take you up on it."

Evans looked over at Frye's rifle, which was leaned up against his gear.

"Is that one of those new-fangled rifles I've heard so much about," Cal said, "with the fancy telescopic sights?"

"Yes, it is."

"Beautiful weapon."

"Thanks."

"Does it shoot as good as they say they do?"

"Yes, it does."

"I plan on getting one of those soon." Cal said.

Frye finished the last of his coffee and began saddling his horse. Then he walked back over to the fire, rolled up his bedroll, and returned to his mount. He lashed the roll behind his saddle.

Cal carefully picked up the rifle, cased it, and took it over to the Deputy, who began to strap it onto his saddle.

"Thanks," Frye said.

"It's the least I can do for a man who fed me," Cal said, before returning to douse the fire with the last of the coffee.

"Hard to make up a mind on an empty belly," the Deputy said, speaking over his shoulder, as he rechecked the cinches on his saddle. "Now that you've eaten, you decide whether you're going with me?"

"I think so," Cal replied.

Smiling, the Deputy turned around from his horse, just as Cal Evans plunged the hot poker deep into his chest.

Frye instinctively reached for his gun, but failed to complete his draw. His lips moved, with no sound being made. Trying to steady himself on his horse, his eyes, wide with disbelief, increasingly grew clouded.

Cal Evans, the man who just killed him, stood there smiling, holding the bloody poker, contented to watch the man die.

As his life's blood drained into the dirt beneath him, Deputy Aiden Frye finally collapsed. He rolled over to face his killer. His last thoughts were of a longing to once again see his wife's face. Then he went forever still.

Quickly removing the deputy's money and gun belt, he dragged the man's body over to low place, behind some rocks. The sun was climbing higher. With his fears of being seen in this place, he covered the body with some brush and stones, in the makeshift grave.

"You say you've had some experience with bad men, Deputy? Not much!"

Once he was safely away from here, the man figured it would be several days before anybody came across the body. Maybe, it would be years before it was discovered. But should the unthinkable actually happen, and someone pursue the deputy's killer, he was confident that nobody else could match his skills with a gun.

The killer laughed to himself, as he gently made his way over to the man's now-skittish horse. Swinging his right leg over the saddle, he looked back over the camp to see if he'd left anything of value.

Mounted on the stolen horse, Cameron Ellis spurred the animal westward.

Chapter Nine

"By the way," Malone said, "you never told me how Nora is doing."

"She's doing just fine," Gain said. "But I'm starting to miss her."

"Well, I was glad to hear that the two of you finally got married."

"Yes," Gain replied. "Long time in coming. Hey! You heard we had a daughter?"

"No, I didn't," Malone said. "That's great. But I kind of figured you two were a little long in the tooth for children."

"Kell!"

"Relax, Gain. I was just kidding with you. Tell me about her."

"Gone all those years like I was, I never knew Nora and me had a daughter. Susan is just a vision. She's beautiful and smart, just like her mother. She's spirited too."

"Like her dad?" Kell said.

Gain laughed "Probably more than I'd like to admit."

"She's married now, married to a fine, young man. He's a lawman too."

"They have any kids?

"Not yet. But they have been talking a lot about it."

"I'm glad to hear it, Gain. You deserve some happiness in your life."

A knock sounded on the door. It was a sound that they had already heard enough times to instantly recognize. As Joe Clements entered the room, he nodded at both of the men, before making his way over to the coffee pot.

"I've been doing a little thinking," Carson said, "since the other night."

"You have?" Malone asked. "Come up with anything?"

"Yes, I did."

"Glad to hear it," said Malone. "It's my best thinking that got us into this mess."

Silently drinking his coffee while cleaning his six-gun, Joe Clements listened silently as Malone and Carson discussed their situation.

As long as Clements had known Kellen Malone, Joe had never seen him act the way he did the day before. Although he probably didn't kill the man, his actions in throwing Ellis off the train were a level of violence Joe had never witnessed in his friend.

He had known Malone to kill people. He had even seen him pull the trigger, when taking a life. But unlike Joe, Malone's killings were always out of principle, never to earn his pay. His victims were rare and necessary.

Joe had killed a number of men, often for the highest bidder. His actions were cold, calculating, and almost clinical. They were never personal.

Malone's treatment of Ellis was brutal, extreme, and deeply personal.

For the first time, Joe realized just how much Malone truly cared for Rachel. He also understood that, should any harm ever come to the woman, Clements didn't want to be standing anywhere between Malone and the one who inflicted that harm.

However, Joe knew, should that day ever come, he would be there with Malone, standing at his side. He knew Malone would do the same for him, as well.

For as different as their backgrounds were, Kellen Malone had proven to be a formidable enemy. More importantly, he was Joe Clements' only friend.

The way I see this," Gain explained, "they've already made a couple of runs at the president. And both of them have been here, on the train."

Malone nodded.

"One of them was in the open, with the riders attacking us directly," Gain continued. "The other was more covert, Ellis holding you at gun point, trying to use you to maneuver his way into Cleveland's room. Everything they've tried has been on the train."

"So, what are you saying?"

"At this point, they haven't been too successful with their plans," said Gain, rubbing his moustache, his mind deep in thought. "The guys trying to kill the president aren't fools. I don't think we can afford to let our guard down; on the other hand, I also don't think they're dumb enough to come at us that way again."

"Oh, I get what you're saying," Malone observed. "On here, we can control the situation. You think we're safe, as long as we stay on the train."

"That's my thinking, exactly."

Turning the idea over in his mind, Kell ran his fingers through his hair. Then he took another sip of his coffee.

"Makes sense to me," Malone said. "What do you think, Joe?"

Clements, who had finished cleaning his gun, was thumbing fresh cartridges into each of the cylinders. He always kept an empty chamber, underneath the hammer. Finally satisfied with the job he had done, Joe holstered the weapon.

"I think the old man is way too smart to be a friend of yours."

Malone laughed. "What about you, Joe. You're a friend of mine, too."

"Not anymore. Ever since I met Carson," Joe said, "I'm thinking of giving a lot more thought to my choice of companions."

"I always like a young man who isn't too stubborn to learn," Carson said, with a laugh.

"If you too keep it up," Malone grumbled, "then Ellis may not be the only man I have to throw off this train."

"Looks like I'd better get started on my rounds," Joe said, feigning a look of fear. "I'll leave you two to catch up on old home week."

The door closed behind him.

"I like that kid," Gain said.

"Me too," Kell muttered. "Just don't let him know it."

***

As she hurriedly carried on the conversation with her daughter, the woman stood there, pretending to clean the window, watching for the young man's return. He was outside now, giving the few remaining table scraps to the chickens.

"Are you sure?" Nora said.

"I'm pretty sure of it, Mama," Susan replied. "I've been sick every morning for the past week."

"When do you plan to tell Slaton?"

"Tonight," Susan said, smoothing down her apron. "I thought I would make him a special dinner, before I break the news."

Despite her fears that their conversation would be overheard, Nora rushed over to her daughter and gave her a big hug. The two of them embraced each other firmly.

"I am so happy for you, dear. I am so happy for the both of you." Overcome by the moment, Nora briefly wiped away a tear. "Gain will be pleased, too."

"Are you sure, Mama?"

"Very much so, dear. Gain has spoken of this many times to me," she explained, softly. "What you don't understand, dear, are his regrets over those many years of being away. The years of not knowing you were his. Those many years of not being a father to you. And to be quite honest, I blame myself for that, also. It was me who never told him.

93

"Many a night, Gain has sat with me," Nora continued, "out on the porch, staring off towards the horizon. Your daddy has told me that he wants to make up for all those years, Susan. He wants to be the influence to his grandchildren that he never was with you."

"But, Mama, I have long since forgiven him for all that."

"But Gain hasn't forgiven himself, Susan. He probably never will."

Susan embraced her once again. "Well, all that matters to me, Mama, is that we *are* a family now."

"A family that is soon to be growing," Nora said with a smile.

Hearing the sounds of a buggy racing towards their house, Nora and Susan rushed to the door. From this distance, it was hard to make out the driver. But it was obvious that the person was in a big hurry.

The buggy pulled to a stop in front of the house. Climbing down from the buggy was a woman. Frantically, the woman jumped down from the buckboard.

"Hello, Sherry," Susan said.

"Oh, hi there, Susan. Nora. Sorry to stop by unannounced."

"Please don't apologize," Susan replied.

"Has Slate seen Aiden?"

"Aiden? I don't think so," Susan said. "Come on inside. Slate should be right in."

"Thank you," Sherry said.

The three women had no more than gotten in the house, when Slate came rushing in the back door. "I thought I heard somebody coming in," Slate said. "They sounded in a hurry. Is everything okay?" Then he spotted the woman sitting at his table. "Oh, it's you, Sherry. How was Aiden's trip?"

"That's what I came here for. He never made it home."

"Never made it home? I got a telegraph from Aiden three days ago. He should have been home yesterday, noon at the latest."

"That's right. He didn't make it home. I'm worried about him, Marshal."

"Let's not jump to any conclusions, Sherry," Slate said. "I'll find him. Would you grab my saddlebags and bedroll, Susan?"

"Sure, Slate," the woman replied, heading to the other room.

Taking time enough to grab his hat and strap on his gun belt, Slate followed her into the other room.

Since his job often required him to leave home at a moment's notice, in pursuit of outlaws or in the transfer of a prisoner, Marshal Slate Callfield always kept an extra bedroll close at hand, with some fresh supplies and provisions in his saddlebags.

Every couple of days, without failure, Susan made sure the gear was in proper order. Like Sherry, she feared and hated those trips, but accepted them as part of his job. But she always did her best to make sure that there was always something special in his gear, a note, some cookies, or a favorite treat, anything to make his time away from her special, and to make him long to quickly return home.

While the two of them went to the other room, Nora did what she could to lessen the woman's fears. Better than anyone, Nora Carson knew the uncertainty the woman must be feeling. She constantly knew the fears of a gunman's wife. Nora poured the woman a cup of coffee and spoke some words of comfort.

"You look worried, Slate," Susan said, only when she knew that they were safely out of the woman's earshot.

"I am worried," he said. "Aiden Frye is as predictable as they come. He doesn't take chances; you can set a watch by the man. If Aiden didn't make it home, then it's because something happened. It could be nothing serious. Maybe the horse threw him or the animal came up lame. But something happened. And I need to go and find him."

Having said that, Slate rushed out the back door to saddle his horse.

A few moments later, Susan met him at the front door, carrying her husband's gear. Slate climbed down from the saddle long enough to grab the saddlebags and lash on the bedroll.

He walked over to the woman and placed his hands on each of her shoulders. "Please try not to worry, Sherry. I will find him. You can count on that."

"Thank you, Marshal," she said, wiping the moisture from her eyes.

Slate nodded and tipped his hat.

"Let's go back inside," Nora said to Sherry, "and let these kids have a moment's privacy."

"Bye to you, Nora," Slate said, before turning back toward his wife. "Susan, I will be back as soon as I can."

He softly took the woman in his arms.

"I'm counting on that, cowboy," she said, doing her best to put on a brave face. "I need to talk to you about something."

"Can it wait until I get back?"

"Sure it can," she said, moving forward to kiss him. Their lips melted together. "You go find Aiden now! We'll talk when you get back."

Slate swung himself into the saddle and urged the animal alongside the porch.

"Jerry is minding the jail today," he said. "I'll swing into town first and get him to go along with me."

He leaned down from his saddle, long enough for one more kiss. After their lips met, Slate smiled, before spurring his horse down the trail.

As Susan watched him disappear into the horizon, she gently rubbed her hand on her belly. "Guess it's just you and me, kid," she said, softly. "Our little announcement will just have to wait."

Chapter Ten

When Malone finally located Jeremiah Langston, the presidential aide was back in the caboose, doing something to the president's lectern. Kell heard the noise of his pounding, long before he went inside.

"Langston, what are you doing?"

Langston, whose manner of dress was nearly always flawless, looked like a man who had been working for hours. He was wearing nothing other than a sweat-stained dress shirt, with the sleeves rolled up to his elbows. There were smudges of dirt on his face and arms. Most of them had already been smeared, by his repeated attempts to wipe the sweat away.

"What does it look like, Kell?" the man impatiently replied. "I'm working on the president's lectern."

Malone laughed. "I can see that. But just what are you doing to it?"

Kell moved around to the other side of the lectern, squatting on his haunches to examine the work that Langston had done.

"There!" the aide said. "That should just about do it."

The inside of the hand-crafted, oaken lectern had been lined with the cast iron doors and plates of several pot bellied stoves, leaving scarcely a place where Malone could see the grains of the wood.

"I see it," Kell muttered. "I'm just not sure what the reason for it is."

"Kellen Malone," Langston said, wiping his face and hands with a towel that used to be white, "I'm shocked at you. I would think a man of your skills would immediately see the purpose of this little invention.

"After having a conversation with Mr. Carson," Langston added, "and upon hearing his credible theory about any future threats on the president, I came up with this idea to shield the man from a sniper's bullet."

"But that will only protect him from any bullets in his chest area," Malone said, scratching his head. "It might also give the president a place to crouch behind, shielding him from any successive gunfire. But what if the first shot's aimed at his head?"

"That's your problem!" Langston said, smugly. "I hired you and Clements to make sure that doesn't happen. And if it does, I'm counting on you to make him miss."

"Glad you aren't putting any pressure on us," Malone said, with a chuckle. "There's one other problem I see with this lectern, too."

"What's that?"

"This thing's going to weigh about three hundred pounds," Kell grumbled. "Who's going to pick it up?"

"That's not my problem, either," Langston replied. "Listen, Kell. Normally, this trip to Sacramento should only take about four days. But because the president wants to address the crowds, and meet the people in every town of any size, we are looking at a trip of approximately two weeks.

"I don't need to tell you, of course, that those plans provide a lot of opportunities for a determined assassin," Langston added, placing his hand on Malone's shoulder. "We cannot afford to take any unnecessary chances with the president's life."

"On that, we're in agreement," Malone said.

"I'm for doing anything we can do to help our odds," said Langston. "By the way, Kell, I never did thank you for bringing Mr. Carson into this enterprise. He seems to be a good man."

"There aren't any better!"

"Indeed. The man probably saved my life," Langston added, "and kept Frances from being kidnapped. Other than you, Kell, I never saw a man draw a gun and fire that fast before."

"Yes, I've seen him in action a couple of times myself."

"What's he like?"

"He's just a man. Pretty much the way he seems. But for all his notoriety, Gain was lonely for a lot of years," Kell explained. "Since he married Nora McDonald, I've never seen the man happier. What about you, Langston. You ever get hitched?"

"Yes, I did. Twice."

"What happened?"

"After the war, I went home and married my childhood sweetheart. We had such a great life together! A couple of years later, when she was expecting our first child, she came down with pneumonia. A week later, the love of my life was dead. Part of me died with them.

"My second wife—I faithfully prayed for the same fate to befall her, as well. That just shows you how well my prayers are answered.

"Ava loved the trappings of Washington, the parties and events, rubbing elbows with those in power," Langston continued. "I later learned that she was rubbing more than elbows with an aspiring state senator. When I caught them together, I nearly beat the man to death with his own cane."

"What happened to her?"

"I later learned that Ava's infidelities didn't stop with me. In the rage of the moment, the senator carried Ava outside and threw her body into a well. His political career stopped at the end of a noose. After that experience, I learned that a woman's beauty was a luxury I could no longer afford."

For several moments, Langston simply stood there, silently admiring his handiwork. "Come on, Malone. We need to get some help, getting this out on the rear platform of the train."

"This sounds like a job," Kell replied, "for somebody who's both strong and stupid."

"You mean like your friend Clements?"

99

"I'll be sure and tell him you said that."

"I'd really rather you didn't, Kell."

***

Thanks to Frye's predictability and already knowing the route he was following, Slate Callfield and Jerry had little trouble in finding his final campsite.

Both of them were good trackers, Jerry only a notch behind the marshal. Often stooping to inspect the ground, Slate carefully studied the campsite.

Off to where the deputy's horse had been tethered, Jerry stooped down to pick up a broken branding iron. He carefully took note of what seemed to be blood, on the end of the rusty steel rod.

"Jerry," he shouted, "come here."

Jerry continued to hold onto the poker, as he followed the sounds of the marshal's voice, over behind the rock. When he saw Slate, the marshal was just removing the last of the brush and rocks from the deputy's body.

"Is that him, Marshal?"

"I wish you would quit calling me that; I've told you before, Jerry. My name is Slate!" he grumbled. Suddenly, Slate was more than a little ashamed that he had responded so harshly. "I'm sorry, Jerry. Guess this thing is getting to me a little, too. Yes, the body is Aiden's."

For several moments, neither of the men said anything. They just silently stared down at the body, a good man gone, married to a young wife, a woman who was now a widow. His only son, Ben, no longer had a father.

"He was stabbed with something," Slate said. "It doesn't look like it was a knife."

"I think I know what killed him," Jerry said, handing the rod over to the marshal. "I found this over by where his horse was tied."

Taking the rod from Jerry, Slate held it over the hole in the dead man's chest. Fearful of doing anything to defile a dead body, Slate hesitated to stick the rod into the wound. It looked to be the right size. The marshal finally decided that was enough.

For the next hour, Slate studied every inch of the campsite. Without being asked, Jerry mounted up, to back-trail the man who visited the deputy's camp.

Thoughtfully, Slate was sitting on a rock, chewing on a piece of jerky when Jerry rode back into camp. The deputy's body was already bound in a blanket and lashed over the saddle of their spare horse.

Jerry immediately took note of Aiden's body on the horse. Silently, he found himself relieved that he wouldn't be responsible for preparing the dead body of his friend for travel.

Dismounting, Jerry sat down on the rock next to the marshal.

"The killer must have taken Aiden's rifle with him," Slate offered.

"I'm not surprised that he did. Beautiful weapon, it was," Jerry said. "Aiden said he always wanted to leave that gun for his boy."

"Let's go over what we know, Jerry. Aiden was all alone here when he first made camp," Slate added. Then, pointing to a place where the stranger had approached. "The killer, appearing to be friendly, came into camp from that direction. I'm sure Aiden invited him in. Then he probably shared some of Aiden's food and coffee, and sat over there, right next to the fire."

"The killer," Jerry said, "didn't have any horse. His tracks started just below the railroad line, like he suddenly came from the train."

"You mean he jumped off?" Slate asked.

"No, Marshal," Jerry replied, looking embarrassed that he had called him by his title once again. "There were no deep heel prints, like those you would expect to find when a man jumped from a moving train.

"I don't know how to explain it, Slate, but it looks to me like he rolled from the train. A better explanation would be—and I know this sounds funny—that it looks like he was thrown off of it. His body just sort of tumbled all the way down the hill. I couldn't find anyplace where his hands dug in, trying to break his fall."

Slate scratched his head at Jerry's explanation; but he harbored no doubts as to the young man's description of the incident. In the past, those who had challenged Jerry's theories were often proven to be wrong.

"Why would someone throw a man off a train, Slate?"

"I suppose it could have been a freeloader, someone riding the train without a ticket."

"But wouldn't he have been conscious when the conductor threw him off?"

"That's the same conclusion I reached," Slate said. "There's something else I'm seeing here that bothers me. Or it's what I'm not seeing."

"You mean other than the fact that there were no signs of a struggle?"

"That bothered me too. This guy's definitely a bad one." Slate said. "But what troubles me is that I can't find Aiden's badge."

"Are you sure?"

"Yes, Jerry. It's nowhere to be found."

"Well you and I both know, Aiden didn't go anywhere without it," Jerry replied. "He was always proud of being a lawman. Why would the killer take it? Did he want some kind of a souvenir of the deed?"

"I sure hope that wasn't the case; for that would make him some special kind of evil," Slate explained. "Then, we would be hearing about a lot more of these kind of murders. No, Jerry, I think there is something more to this. I'm afraid he may have a certain reason to pose as a lawman."

"Why would he want to do that?"

"Maybe he wants to break somebody out of jail, while impersonating a lawman. Maybe wearing a badge will keep anybody from questioning his actions, or looking into his motives. I don't know for sure what his reason is, Jerry; but it's darned sure I'm going to try and stop whatever he has in mind!"

"So, we're going after him, Slate?"

"No, Jerry. I'm going after him. You're going to take the body back to town. Tell Aiden's wife that I'm going to find the man who killed her husband."

"And our friend," Jerry added.

"Yes, he was, Jerry." Slate placed his hand on the young man's shoulder. "I'm putting you in charge until I get back."

"But, Slate," he blustered, "do you really think I'm ready for all that?"

"I wouldn't ask you, Jerry, unless I thought you were ready. If you need any help, ask Phil, over at the general store, to lend you a hand. He's a good man."

"Okay, Slate," he said, his voice trembling in fear and excitement. "Is there anything else you want me to do?"

"Yes, there is. After you get the body home and talk to Mrs. Frye, I want you to ride out to my place. Please let Susan know what I am doing. Tell her not to worry."

"Telling a woman not to worry, does that really work, Slate?"

In spite of their discovery of these grisly events, Slaton laughed out loud. "No, it doesn't really help much. It's just something that you do anyway," he replied. "How'd you ever come to know so much about women, Jerry?"

"My mom was a woman," he said, soberly.

"That she was," Slate said, with a smile.

The two men climbed into their saddles. Jerry tied the reins of the extra pack horse, carrying Frye's body, to his horse's saddle horn. Then he reined his horse around, firmly shaking the marshal's outstretched hand.

"You can count on me, Slate. I'll do my best to not betray your confidence in me."

"I'm sure of that. Is there anything else, Jerry?"

"Just one more thing. You might need this," Jerry replied, handing the marshal the Sharps rifle that he always carried on his saddle.

"Thank you, Jerry."

Gratefully, Slaton Callfield accepted the weapon, checked the action, and proceeded to shove it down into his empty rifle scabbard.

Reaching deep into his coat pocket, Jerry came out with a handful of rifle cartridges. Those, he also placed in Slate's hand. "Just in case."

The marshal nodded.

"You be careful, Slate. Whoever done this *is* a special kind of evil."

As Slate Callfield watched the young man ride away, he carefully checked his six-gun. "A special kind of evil," he muttered underneath his breath. "That he is, Jerry."

Chapter Eleven

It was almost ten o'clock when a lone rider walked his horse up the street of Cheyenne. Thirsty, hungry, and desperately in need of a bath, the man had slept very little in the past couple days.

The town of Cheyenne was clearly in a festive mood. The boardwalks were filled with visitors and townspeople, rushing here and there. Well-dressed men and women, mounted on horses and riding in buggies, filled the dusty, wind-swept, city streets.

American flags and colorful patriotic buntings were hung from every balcony, railing, and storefront window. Red, white, and blue streamers also hung from the electric lamp posts, whose incandescent lamps illuminated the streets at night, making Cheyenne one of the most the sophisticated cities west of the Mississippi.

Seeing the train depot in front of him, the man deliberately looked around, turning in his saddle, carefully studying the surrounding landscape, buildings, and rooftops. He immediately saw a couple of excellent prospects for his plans.

"You must be here to see the president," one of the passersby said to him.

"Yes, I am, friend."

"Couldn't have picked a better day for it," the man added, as he walked down the boardwalk, which was parallel to the street.

"So, I take it the train hasn't arrived yet?"

"No, it hasn't. President Cleveland isn't supposed to be here for about six hours."

"That's good," the rider said. "Maybe it will give me time to clean up a little."

"I hope you enjoy your stay in Cheyenne, friend."

"So do I."

"My name's Benson."

"You can call me Cam."

"You plan on staying long, Cam?"

"No longer than it takes to do what I came here for."

"Well, it was good meeting you, stranger" the man replied. "Maybe I'll see you there later, when the president's speaking."

"I doubt you'll see me."

"I guess you've got a point. There's likely to be quite a crowd there." The man said, pausing on the boardwalk, before entering the barber's shop. "It was good to meet you, Cam."

"Same here," Cam Ellis replied, briefly tipping his hat. "The pleasure was all mine."

As he urged his stolen horse on down the street, Ellis had to smile to himself. In just a few brief moments of seemingly-polite conversation, the gunman had successfully gleaned a wealth of useful information.

By talking to the stranger as he rode alongside him on the street, Cam wasn't forced to ask a lot of specific questions. He drew no attention to himself. In addition, the crucial information he acquired raised no undue suspicions as to his motives.

Ellis drew rein in the front of the Inter-Ocean Hotel, at precisely the same time as the Deadwood Stage, carrying a load of hopeful gold seekers, departed for the promise of fortune in Dakota's Black Hills.

Lodging place to presidents and other notables, the Inter-Ocean was the largest hotel in the city. The establishment was also one of the most prominent hotels in the West.

The founder of this hotel and a similar one in Denver was Barney Ford, a former slave, who first made his way to Chicago after escaping his Virginia slave holders. He later traveled to Nicaragua, where he opened his first hotel.

Longing for the promise of riches in the Colorado goldfields, Barney was unable to take the stage because he was a black man. Unshackled by circumstances or the color of his skin, the relentless former slave reached the Colorado mines by way of a wagon train, signing on with the travelers as a barber.

Ford's gold claim was later stolen from him by unscrupulous, white officials. And although they personally never found any gold there, apparently Barney escaped with enough gold dust to bankroll his next round of successful business investments.

Ellis tied his horse to the hitching rail, ducked under, and made his way inside the Inter-Ocean. Over his shoulder, he carried the stolen rifle and saddlebags.

As the gunman approached the desk, the aged, black caretaker spoke to him. "May I help you, sir?"

"I need a room for a couple of hours," Cam said. "Been riding for days to get here in time for the president's visit."

"I'm sorry, but I don't have any."

"You care to see the color of my money first?" said Ellis.

"No, it's not that, sir. I would love to rent you a room, if I had any to let. There just aren't any vacancies," he said. Then he pointed to a comfortable sofa in the corner of the hotel's lobby. "For two bits, I'll let you catch some sleep on the sofa. If you let me know when to wake you, I will see that you get up."

"You have yourself a deal," Cam said, with an easy smile. But as quickly as the smile came, it was gone. Instantly, his face turned as sober as a judge. "Don't let me sleep any longer than two hours. And make sure I am not disturbed. Do you understand?"

"I understand you want a place to sleep, sir," the black man said. "But you also need to understand that you do not make the rules at the Inter-Ocean. Mr. Ford does!"

"Maybe I should have you horse-whipped," Ellis replied.

"I've already been horse whipped, mister. And it isn't going to happen again," the black man softly stated, removing a sawed-off shotgun from underneath the counter. He pointed both barrels at the gunman and eared back the triggers. "Now, if you care to mind your manners, sir, you are more than welcome to sleep here in the lobby.

"But if you choose to continue your impertinence, then you are welcome to immediately leave this establishment," the elderly black man, genteelly stated. "If you care to reach for your gun, then there are plenty of vacancies in hell. And I am certain that a man like yourself will find the place to your liking. Now which will it be, sir?"

Cam smiled, knowing that the deck was clearly stacked against him. Under normal circumstances, he might have chosen to push the situation. However, his plans might be thwarted if he was to become embroiled in a shooting incident.

In addition, he grudgingly had to admire the elderly black man's spirit. It was obvious that the man had been a former slave. Moreover, he knew it took a real measure of courage to escape the bonds of slavery.

At this point, Ellis doubted that the elderly gentleman truly feared him; he doubted that the man truly feared anyone.

"Perhaps I was, as you say, a bit impertinent," Cam said, "I believe I will take the sofa."

Upon hearing the answer, the old man's gentle smile returned. Slowly, he released the hammers on the shotgun. "I trust you will be more than satisfied with the accommodations, sir. Please enjoy your nap."

Ellis reached into his pocket and slapped down a couple of bits on the counter. He walked over to the sofa and sat down. Using the saddlebags for a pillow, and leaving his booted feet hanging over the opposite armrest, Cam stretched out his weary body. The rifle, he gently placed on the floor beside him. The moment his head touched down, Ellis was sound asleep.

Silently, the elderly, black caretaker watched the man getting comfortable. Something in the stranger's eyes reminded him of his past life in Alabama. He looked at the hotel's fine grandfather clock and carefully noted the time.

"No more than two hours," he muttered, underneath his breath. A question lingered in his mind. He wondered what interest a man such as this would have in seeing the president.

He watched Ellis for a time, before returning to his duties.

***

"I've got a bad feeling about this, Langston" Kell said. "Couldn't we just cancel this appearance and go on to Sacramento?"

"As much as it pains me to say this, sir," Langston replied, looking at the president, "I happen to agree with Malone on this one."

"No, we can't," Cleveland said, lighting a cigar. "Care to join me?"

Malone and Langston both passed on the offer.

"This appearance has been planned for quite some time," he continued. "The people are counting on us being there. And besides, you have already taken every precaution. I saw the work you did on the lectern."

"But nobody can guarantee that all those precautions will be successful," Langston said.

"That is my point, exactly," the president replied. "There are no guarantees in this life, except for the fact that none of us are getting out of it alive."

"Would you consider cancelling your appearance?"

"I already did consider it, Jeremiah," he replied, with a smile. "Frances and I decided against it.

"Listen, Kell. And, Jeremiah, you need to hear this too," said the president. "I came to the conclusion a long time ago that officeholders are the agents of the people, not their masters.

"The people who sent this administration to Washington have a right to look us in the eye, to determine if we remain worthy of their confidence. Along with that, we have a responsibility to make ourselves available to them, so they ultimately can make those determinations." He took another puff from the cigar. "I will not cower behind my protectors, at the expense of my duties."

Although he was increasingly frustrated by his inability to talk some sense into the president, Malone admired the man's unflinching courage.

"I will not change my plans."

"Even if those plans get you killed?" Kell asked.

"Perhaps I can find another way to explain it you," Cleveland said. "I know all about your attempts to clear your name, Kell, after you were released from prison."

"So?" Malone blustered. "I can't see what that has to do with what we're talking about?"

"Then I will explain it to you," the president said. "When you were engaged in those efforts, didn't you understand that there would be some risk involved in your plans?"

"Of course I did?"

"Did you also know, Mr. Malone, that there were people out there who didn't want you to succeed in your plans?'

"Yes," he said. "But it made no difference to me."

"Yet, despite those obvious dangers and the deliberate efforts by others to impede your goals, you chose to do it anyway. Why is that, Kell?"

"I don't know," Malone declared. "I just thought it was the right thing to do."

"Then why would you expect any less of me, sir? After all," Cleveland added, "what is the point of being elected or re-elected, unless you stand for something?

"And you, Jeremiah, didn't you occasionally fear for your life on the battlefield?" Cleveland said. "But you chose to follow your orders anyway. Why is that?"

Unable to come up with a reasonable response, Langston simply hung his head.

Cleveland stubbed out the remainder of his cigar, before saying anything else. "The right thing to do, you say, those five words should be the mission of every public servant."

"You are certainly a persuasive man, sir," Kell said, with a smile. "Did you ever consider running for high elective office?"

"Perhaps I shall," Cleveland stated.

Just about that time, the train whistle sounded on their approach to the next stop on their tour. Making his way past the soldiers stationed outside the door, the porter entered the president's room. The man was accompanied by Joe Clements and Gain Carson.

"Mr. President," the porter said, "we are about to make a brief stop in Cheyenne. If you will look out the window, you will see that there is a big crowd waiting to see you, sir. For your safety, I ask that you remain seated until the train comes fully to a stop. Please enjoy your stay."

After the porter left the president's room, Malone looked at Langston and Clements. "Waiting until the train comes fully to a stop," Kell said, "I wish that was all we had to do to keep the man safe."

President Cleveland threw back his head in laughter at the remark.

"What do you want me to do, Kell?" Clements said.

"Joe, I want you and Gain on top of the train, standing above the crowd," Malone said. "If anybody even looks like they're raising a gun, I want you to take them out."

"Far be it from me to question your wisdom, Kell," Gain said, "but doesn't standing on top of the train make us really easy targets?"

"I've already thought about that," Kell said.

"You hear that, Joe?" Gain muttered. "Kell has thought about it. I feel much better now. Don't you, Joe?"

"Yeah," Clements replied. "Malone has thought about it. That should clear up any remaining doubts I might have had."

"Will you two shut up for a minute?" Kell grumbled. "If anybody takes a shot at either of you, then they won't ever get a chance at assassinating President Cleveland."

"That's supposed to make me feel better?" Carson said. "Well, just what are you going to be doing while we're playing sitting ducks?"

"I'm going to try to make the killer miss his first shot," Malone replied, "unless of course, the man decides to use it on one of you."

"Listen, gentlemen, I don't find anything funny about this," Langston declared. "This is serious business we're engaged in, trying to protect the president's life."

"Spoken like a man who won't be part of the shooting gallery," Joe said.

"That's enough out of you, Mr. Clements." Langston replied.

"That's enough out of all of you," the president stated. "Do I need to remind you again that our enemies are not on the train? They are outside." Cleveland briefly looked at all of those assembled in the room. "Are you men ready? I have a speech to make."

"Give the two of us a couple of minutes," Joe said, "to get to our places on top of the caboose."

"Maybe you ought to take a long gun with you," Malone added.

Joe shook his head as he patted his holster. "No, Kell. I'm good with this."

"I'm fine, too" Gain replied.

"Good luck to you," Malone said.

"Don't worry about us, boy," Gain said. "We'll be fine."

"Yeah," Joe said. "Kell's already thought about it."

Chapter Twelve

It had been a hard, brutal trail for the young marshal, relentlessly following Aiden Frye's killer into the town of Cheyenne.

Slate Callfield didn't find the trail particularly hard to follow. It didn't appear that the killer had been making any real efforts to hide his tracks. Perhaps the man didn't know anyone was following him; perhaps he simply didn't care. Most of Slate's troubles had rested in the fact that Frye's killer was still several hours ahead of him.

Although he tried to close the gap by riding without sleep and rarely stopping to eat, Slate had managed to gain some valuable time on the man. Ultimately, He feared it wouldn't be enough. Removing the watch from his vest pocket, the young marshal could see it was nearly three o'clock in the afternoon.

Slate realized that he was still four or five hours behind the man. Looking at the western sky, he saw the ominous storm clouds gathering over the mountains. Slate cursed softly. The coming rains would wipe out any last traces of the killer's trail.

For the first time, Slate feared that Aiden Frye's killer would go unpunished.

Living most of his life in small cattle towns, Callfield had never seen a place with so many modern conveniences. In fact, he never really believed that such places truly existed in the West. Under any other circumstances, Slate would have spent more time admiring the surroundings. Now, he could think only of catching a killer.

With all of the decorations that adorned the street, he could see that the town was getting ready for some kind of celebration. That meant that there would be a lot of strangers in the town, making it a lot more difficult to once again locate the tracks of the deputy's killer.

Then he saw it, the deputy's horse.

***

When Cameron Ellis woke from his sleep, he felt unusually refreshed. Looking at the hotel clock, he let out with a string of foul oaths, heard by everybody in the lobby. Then he caught himself. He had slept for three hours.

Looking over at the hotel clerk, the man smugly returned Cam's gaze. The aged, black man was smiling from ear to ear. Cam briefly considered putting a bullet through the man's skull. But for the sake of his mission, Ellis decided against it.

His initial plan called for him to get a bath, a shave, and a haircut. That would have been followed by a fine meal, a good cigar, and a warm shot of whiskey. Then he would carefully take the time to scout out the perfect location to carry out his purpose.

Unfortunately, the extra hour's sleep required Cam to eliminate some of those things from his plan. Cleanliness drew the short straw.

If everything else went according to plan, in the commotion that was likely to ensue, Ellis calmly decided that he would return to the hotel lobby. Then, with everyone's attention directed elsewhere, Cam would kill the smug hotel clerk.

The thought brought a smile to his dirty, unshaven face.

Brushing the trail dust off his clothes the best he could. Ellis made his way into the restaurant. His mind was on a big, juicy steak and some hard liquor.

Since he had ridden the horse so hard for the past few days, Cam figured the stolen animal was nearly spent. His need for a quick and successful escape would call for a fresh mount. The animal would stay behind; he would steal another.

Upon finishing his first good meal in days, Cam briefly stopped by the general store, and came out of the place with a small package wrapped in string. Then he removed the rifle and its scabbard from his saddle.

Carrying the two items, Ellis whistled softly, as he started down the street. Trying to blend into the scenery and bustle of the busy city, he spoke kindly and tipped his hat to each of the people who passed him there.

Making his way down to the train depot, Ellis carefully scouted the two locations he noted, upon his arrival in Cheyenne that morning. Finally, he settled on a location on a nearby rooftop. The place provided a great field of fire. Checking his watch, he saw it was almost two hours before the train's arrival.

It would be a long wait. But in order to keep from being spotted, it was necessary for Cam to be in place early. It also didn't hurt that Ellis enjoyed his work. He loved stalking a victim; Cam treasured the moments leading up to the kill.

In fact, he found it much more satisfying than actually pulling the trigger.

On the ground, people were already starting to gather around. Cam untied the package, removing the box of shells, the tobacco, and the rolling papers. After opening the box of shells and sticking several of them in his pocket, he began to roll several cigarettes, something that would help him pass the time.

Then he carefully removed the rifle from its case, before opening the breech. Cam removed the old cartridge and replaced it with a fresh one. A job done well was a job done right.

Getting in a prone position, he sighted down the telescopic sight at the place where the train would stop. Satisfied with his positioning, Cam lit a cigarette and settled down to wait.

Then he smiled.

The president would never know what hit him. One shot is all it would take. Best of all, Kellen Malone and Joe Clements could do absolutely nothing to stop him.

And if he got real lucky, before he escaped, he might just have enough time to put his second shot into the body of Kellen Malone

**

When Slate saw Aiden's horse, his first thought was that the killer had stolen another horse and ridden out of town. With the rains coming, he knew the killer might escape.

The thought of it left a great big, hollow place in his gut.

He drew rein in front of the general store, leaving his animal ground hitched. Hoping to find some more information, but not expecting much, Slate went inside.

"Howdy, stranger," the storekeeper said. "You here for the festivities?"

"What festivities?"

"President Cleveland's visit," he declared. "Didn't figure there was anyone who hadn't heard of it."

"I guess I didn't," Slate said.

"He should be in town just about any time now. You may just be my last customer, friend. I'm planning to close the store and go down there, myself."

The stranger pulled back his coat to reveal a badge. "I'm Marshal Slate Callfield. I'm looking for the man who was riding that horse outside your store. He might have been carrying a rifle, one of them with the new telescopic sights."

"Yes, Marshal, I saw that man. He was just here a little while ago."

"Really?" Slate asked, unable to believe his good fortune.

"Yes, I remember him well. He bought a box of rifle shells."

"Rifle shells, you say?

"Yes," the man replied. He pointed to another box on the shelf just over his right shoulder. "Rifle shells and some cigarette makings. Seemed like a nice guy to me."

"Well, he isn't a nice man!" Slate fumed. "He isn't a nice man at all. The guy is a snake and a cold-blooded killer. He murdered a friend of mine, a lawman who was guilty of nothing other than inviting a hungry stranger to his fire."

"I'm sorry to hear that, Marshal," the storekeeper said. "What can I do to help you?"

"You wouldn't happen to know where the man went, would you?"

"No, I don't, Marshal. He started down the street toward the railroad station. I just figured he was going to see the president, like most everybody else in town."

"Can you describe the man?"

"He was a tall, thin galoot. Dark eyed. Also, he was sporting a couple day's growth of beard," the storekeeper said. "Except for a white shirt, he was dressed in black. His clothes looked kind of tattered and stained.

"Looked like he did his best to appear clean, but he looked like a man who'd been rolling around on the ground recently. That's just about all I remember."

"You sure that's all?"

"Yes, I'm sure," the storekeeper replied. "There was one other thing. But it may have been nothing."

"What was that?"

"When he walked in my store, I almost swore I heard Joe Benson call him Cam. But I can't be sure. That name mean anything to you, Marshal?"

"No, it doesn't. But maybe it gives me someplace to start. Besides, it's a lot more than I had when I walked in here."

"Anything else I can get you?"

"No," Slate said, turning to leave the store. "You've been a big help."

"Glad I could help you," the storekeeper said, following him outside. At the door, he put a *Closed* sign in the window. "Hope you find your man, Marshal."

"So do I," Slate said.

Callfield watched the man leave, the storekeeper hurrying down the street to see the president. Unsure of where to go next, Slate climbed back into the saddle.

Taking a long pull from his canteen, Slate decided to check out the festivities at the train depot. If the man hadn't already left town, maybe he would get lucky.

Just then, he heard the whistle of a distant train.

Chapter Thirteen

After his unsuccessful attempt to hire Joe Clements to kill Kellen Malone, Vincent Fielding made no effort to return to San Francisco. He was perfectly content to stay behind in Colorado.

If their attempts to assassinate the president were ever discovered, then Fielding thought the best course of action was to be far away from the scene of the crime. Leave it to his co-conspirators, Wilson Stonegate and Joseph Blakemore, to remain in their California offices.

At this time, he wanted nothing to do with the state. Moreover, there was nothing he could do in San Francisco that couldn't be accomplished equally as well from his comfortable Denver office.

There was also another reason to remain behind, a woman.

Fielding's sources of information were many and far reaching. Less than four hours after the riders attacked the train, Vincent had already learned about the unsuccessful attempt on the president's life. He knew the plan was the brainchild of Wilson Stonegate.

Although the assault on the train had been foolhardy and poorly planned, Fielding grudgingly admired Stonegate's initiative. He liked a man who knew what he wanted, and would stop at nothing to get it.

In addition, Vincent was increasingly growing concerned by Joseph Blakemore's apparent reluctance to take the steps necessary to preserve their fortunes. If the man continued to display these signs of cold feet, then Blakemore might prove to be a liability.

Cleveland's policies were a direct threat to their wealth. In Fielding's mind, there was no question that the man had to be stopped, by any means possible.

His hope still rested in Cameron Ellis.

Although he was very much aware that the man had been thrown from the train, Fielding had yet to learn if his trouble shooter was still alive.

However, once Cameron Ellis had been paid for a job, a six-foot parcel of earth was the only thing that would keep the gunman from finishing the job. The man was professional; he was relentless. Ellis was like a machine. He killed without conscience or hesitation.

Fielding's money was on Cam Ellis.

As he sat in front of the saloon, waiting for the departure of one of the saloon gals, Fielding checked the time on his watch. After carefully watching her all week, Vincent had become acquainted with the woman's schedule.

The saloon girl had first caught his eye the day he met with Joe Clements. He had wanted the woman ever since that time. Tonight, he would have her.

Just like clockwork, the woman finally left the saloon alone, at the end of her shift. As usual, the fabric of her clothes did little to hide the appealing form of the woman beneath them.

"Hello, Jenny," Vincent said, rising to his feet and tipping his hat.

"How are you, Mr. Fielding?"

"Just fine, ma'am. But I would be pleased if you would call me Vincent," he said, confident that no woman could resist his charming smile and polite conversation. "Perhaps you would care to join me for drink."

"I would be glad to share a drink with you, Mr. Fielding, if you will just catch me when I am working."

"Well, I had something a little more private in mind," he said, stepping to one side in order to block her path, "maybe over at my office."

"I am flattered by the offer," she said. "But I don't think so."

"Come on, Jenny. Have a drink with me."

"I said no, Mr. Fielding. Now I ask you to let me go on my way," Jenny replied, trying to push past the man.

"The hell you will!"

Unable to imagine that any woman would turn down a man of his obvious status, Fielding would not let her pass. Viciously, he grabbed her arm and pulled her up against him. His arm slipped around her waist.

"Now, that's more like it," he said. "I think we ought to go to your room."

Jenny fought to break free of his grip, but his strength was far too much for her. "Please let me go, Mr. Fielding."

Several people saw Fielding struggling with the woman. A number of them thought it was little more than a lover's quarrel or the drunken, playful affections of a man with a sporting girl from the saloon.

A couple of others recognized Vincent Fielding. They knew the woman was being harassed. But their natural inclination to intercede was restrained by their fear of the man's great wealth and power. They also feared the gunmen he often had in his employment.

"I have to tell you that I've been thinking of being alone with you for a long time, Jenny."

"Well, it's not going to happen," she insisted, trying to push herself away from the man's grip on her.

"Why not?"

"It just isn't!"

"Listen, Jenny," he said, the anger flaring in his eyes. "You're nothing more than another cheap saloon harlot. You've been with others. Now you'll be with me!"

He started to pull her along.

"Maybe so," she said. "But that was before. I don't do that anymore."

"Saving yourself for Clements, I guess."

"Joe loves me!"

"I suppose he does," Vincent blustered. "I might love you, too, Jenny, especially after I've had my way with you."

"It's not like that," she insisted.

"Why would any decent woman let a scar-faced killer, like Skull Clements, touch her?" Greedily, Fielding pulled her closer, forcing his lips down upon hers. "Don't you try to tell me you didn't like that!"

Finally managing to free her arm, Jenny slapped him across the face. "Let go of me, you filthy pig."

A man used to having his way, Fielding couldn't comprehend the idea that any woman would dare to choose a man like Clements over him. The only thing larger than his pocketbook was the man's vanity. And unrestrained power often drives away a man's inhibitions.

Fielding drew the woman to him again, kissing her one more time. Jenny continued to struggle, desperate to break free of his grip.

"Let her go, mister!"

The speaker was the young caretaker at the saloon. Blessed with an abundance of kindness, but little in the way of intelligence, Billy cleaned up the saloon every night at closing time.

Standing six feet, five inches tall, he towered over most of the men in town. However, the young man was as gentle as his stature was imposing. All of the ladies at the saloon knew him; all of the ladies liked him. He was the sweet, little brother that most of them had or wanted.

Some people speculated that Billy spent too much time in the womb on the day of his birth. The idea was given some credibility, because his mother died during the process.

"Please let her go," Billy insisted, lightly tapping Vincent on the shoulder.

"Now, you just go on your way, Billy," Fielding said. "This is between me and the lady. Do you understand?"

"I understand that Miss Jenny has asked you to stop."

Reacting to the young man's interruption like he would to the irritation of a troublesome house fly, Fielding attempted to brush the young man away. "Get out of here, dummy! The woman and I want to be alone."

Wise enough to understand that his intelligence was not equal to that of others around him, Billy was still sensitive to the issue. He hated to be called dumb or stupid. Moreover, it was the only situation that would bring the sweet young man to a level of violence.

"Please don't call me dumb, sir."

While still holding onto Jenny's wrist, Fielding used his free hand to push the young man away. "You don't know who you are messing with, kid. Just stay out of my business."

Billy was insistent. "Then turn loose of Miss Jenny!"

This time, Fielding fully released his grip on the woman. An imposing figure of a man, himself, Vincent believed Billy was no match for him in strength or intellect. Moreover, he held nothing but contempt for anyone who attempted to thwart his purposes.

"This is the last time I'm telling you, dummy. Get away from me!" Vincent said, throwing a right hand at the saloon's caretaker.

Moving with the speed and finesse of a trained boxer, Billy ducked under the blow. Then he stabbed a left to Fielding's jaw. Grabbing the man by the front of his shirt, Billy flung his unconscious body into the dusty street.

"Are you okay, Miss Jenny?"

"Yes, I am, Billy. And thank you," Jenny said. "I just wish you had stayed out of this."

"I couldn't let him hurt you."

"I know that, Billy. That's one of the things that makes you so sweet." Standing on her tip-toes, Jenny lightly kissed Billy on the cheek.

The action brought a blush to the young man's face. "We need to get out of here. Would you care to walk me home?"

"Sure I would."

As the two of them started down the street, Jenny said, "Do you have to work tonight."

"Yes."

"Well, please be careful this evening, Billy. Fielding is a bad man. He might want to get even with you."

"Okay, Miss Jenny. I am always careful. I haven't broken any of the glasses since last month. And I cleaned it up so good, you couldn't even tell it ever happened."

"That's nice, Billy," Jenny replied.

Chapter Fourteen

The train's whistle sounded one more time as it approached the station.

As the storm clouds began to appear on the horizon, the President of the United States had once again come to Cheyenne.

Slate drew rein at the train depot just about the time the locomotive came to a complete stop. Then he saw the huge crowd of people gathered to see the president. The sight of it brought a foul oath to his lips.

He wondered how he would ever find Frye's killer in this crowd.

Passengers began disembarking from off the train; others clamored to get aboard the locomotive. And although they continued to scurry to their destinations, there was clearly no need to rush. The train wouldn't be departing the station again until President Cleveland delivered his speech and shook a few hands.

Still mounted on horseback at the back of the assembled throng, Slate carefully scanned the crowd. He tried to take note of each and every person among the political well-wishers. At the same time, he knew the effort was likely to be futile.

If the man was somewhere in this crowd, it would be nearly impossible for Slate to spot him. Perhaps that was the killer's ultimate purpose.

Maybe he realized there was somebody closely following his trail. Then, in an effort to lose his pursuers, he wisely chose to blend in with the crowd. Perhaps it was only a lucky break on the part of the killer.

There were so many questions in the young marshal's mind. Would the killer return for his horse? What if he had already left town on another stolen horse? How would he ever pick up the killer's trail again? And what if the killer decided to get on the train?

Slate finally just admitted to himself that he was all out of ideas.

It was obvious to Slate that the pair of armed men, who climbed atop the train, were stationed there to protect the president. He also noticed that one of them looked vaguely familiar to him. Closer observation revealed the man on the left to be someone he knew, his father-in-law, Gain Carson.

Slate knew that Gain had gone to help a friend that he'd never met, someone named Kellen Malone. It was only now that he learned what Susan's father was doing to help the man. Gain was a bodyguard for President Cleveland.

Slate knew his daughter would be so proud of him.

Just about the time Slate started to wave at Carson, the president made his way out to the lectern at the rear of the caboose. As Cleveland waved at the crowd, they broke out into a thunder of cheers and applause.

Behind the president, on one side, was a well-dressed man with a walrus mustache. Also stationed there, was a tall man, with a tied-down six-gun. Although most of his attention seemed to be focused on the president, it was obvious that he also was keeping a close eye on the spectators.

Standing behind the president, on the other side, were a couple of attractive young women. Slate figured one of them was the president's wife. He had no idea who the other woman might be.

Carson and the other man, the bodyguards on top of the train, were actively scanning the crowd for any threat on the president's life.

Still on horseback, Callfield failed to see the other man, the man on the rooftop, who was directing all of his attention on Cleveland.

After acknowledging the cheers of the crowd, the president held his arms in the air, motioning them to stop their ovation.

"Thank you, ladies and gentlemen," the president said. "It's good to be in Cheyenne!"

Once again, the throng of people erupted into an ovation. The president smiled and waited for some silence before he continued.

Momentarily forgetting about his need to catch his deputy's killer, Slaton decided to take a few brief moments to listen to the president's speech.

"A government for the people," Cleveland stated, "must depend for its success on the intelligence, the morality, the justice, and the interest of the people themselves." As the outstanding orator spoke, the president did his best to stare each person in the eye. "But this government also requires that the people have a right to demand the same things of those who would seek to lead them.

"There surely is no difference in his duties and obligations," Cleveland continued, "whether a person is entrusted with the money of one man or many. And yet it sometimes appears as though the office holder assumes that a different rule of fidelity prevails between him and the taxpayer."

At that very moment, Cameron Ellis began raising the rifle. He briefly took a moment to put the scope's crosshairs on each of the men on top of the train. Cam smiled to himself, realizing that he had only to squeeze the trigger to end the career of gunman, Skull Clements.

Then he lowered his aim, moving the gun to cover Kellen Malone. Despite the fact he was fully committed to his mission, Cam was conflicted between his desires and his duty. With every stroke of his being, Ellis resisted his selfish urge to kill the man.

Although it was possible that Ellis might get a second shot, he also knew it would be foolish to assume that he could count on getting more than one.

President Cleveland *was* the target.

Although he was widely regarded as an expert with a six-gun, Ellis was equally comfortable with a long gun. Cam smiled at the thought of the gun's owner. Aiden Frye might have been a fool, he thought, but the man definitely knew his weapons. The gun was one the finest he had ever seen

As he settled into his final, prone shooting position, Cam began to position the crosshairs on the president's upper chest. Then he waited for the precise moment. Satisfied with the moment, Ellis began to take up slack in the trigger...

As the president continued his speech, Slate suddenly noticed some movement from a nearby rooftop. Looking again, he saw it was a man, a man with a scoped rifle.

Immediately, Slate decided that this must be the man he was seeking, the man who killed his friend. This was the murderer, the man who stole Aiden's rifle, who was training his weapon on the president.

Seeing that the men on top of the caboose had failed to notice the gunman, Slate quickly began to reach for the Sharps. Bringing the gun to his shoulder, he took aim at the sniper on the roof.

Then he carefully began to squeeze the trigger...

From his perch on top of the train, Joe Clements was confident that he saw a potential assassin, at the back of the crowd, removing a rifle from the scabbard. The young man brought the Sharps to his shoulder, beginning to take aim, apparently in their direction.

Palming his gun with a speed that was rarely seen in the West, Clements eared back the hammer as he drew. Then he brought the gun level.

"Gun!" he shouted.

Upon hearing those words, Kell sprinted, then dived towards the president, desperately hoping to cover the man with his own body, pushing him out of the line of fire.

Scarcely a split second behind Clements, Gain saw the young man with the Sharps. He immediately recognized the shooter as his son-in-law. Unsure of Slate's motives, Gain instinctively knew that the young lawman wasn't aiming at them.

But Gain knew that Joe Clements had no way of knowing that fact and his gun had already cleared leather.

As the events began to unfold around him, the seconds passing like lightning bolts, there was no time to shout. There was no way to stay Joe's hand. Gain was only helpless to watch what might be the last moments of the young man's life.

Taking aim at the mounted young man with the rifle, Clements' finger began to tense on the trigger…

At nearly the same moment, three shots sounded as one, setting off a sequence of events that absolutely nobody could have predicted.

As Joe's gun flamed in his hand at the man astride the horse, the animal suddenly turned its head. The deadly slug from Clements' gun, meant for Slate Callfield, struck the marshal's horse in the left eye.

This caused the animal to go down, loosing its rider from the saddle.

That action caused Callfield's bullet to miss its mark, errantly striking the scope on Cam's rifle. This, in turn, caused the sniper's rifle bullet to go off target, landing three inches below its intended mark.

Despite Malone's quick actions to protect the president's life, Cam's slug would still have mortally wounded the man. Only the cast iron plating in the lectern saved his life. As the bullet tore its wicked path through the lumber of the lectern, it struck the cast iron with a loud metallic ping.

Only a brief moment behind Malone, Langston bravely moved to cover the president, pushing Malone aside.

"I'll get him back in the car, Malone," Langston shouted, shielding the president with his body. "You get the killer."

As she saw her husband reacting to the danger, Rachel Malone began to shove the president's wife back towards the doorway, out of the line of fire.

Hearing the sound of gunfire and immediately leaving his post, Denton Turner came rushing to the rear of the train. Seeing the women through the window, he threw open the door, grabbed their arms, and jerked the pair of women inside the safety of the caboose.

Having failed in his attempt on the president's life, Cam Ellis dropped the now-useless rifle. The weapon slid down the roof, clattering to the ground below.

Sensing the true danger to the president, Gain immediately began shooting at the man on the rooftop. Joe Clements, unable to get a second shot at the man on the downed horse, instantly joined him in the shooting.

At the first sounds of gunfire, there was chaos throughout the city. Fear ruled the day. Men, women, and children began to flee the train yard. The weak and elderly were often knocked down, their bodies trampled, as others raced to get away from the shooting.

There was screaming and shouting, mothers calling out for their children who had been separated from their arms. Women and children were crying. Men were cursing. The pungent smell of gun smoke filled the air. All around them, it was pandemonium.

Some of the men, army veterans and those routinely familiar with the gun, were outraged that anyone would once again try to brazenly kill their president. They also began to fire their guns at the man on the rooftop.

Confident that the man on the roof was the killer of Aiden Frye, Slate Callfield also triggered his gun at the outlaw. Although he had the best angle on the man, the crowds pushing past him made it impossible to steady his arm or get any more than one shot.

Cameron Ellis scrambled to get away, bullets striking the roof all around him. One of them burned his side and creased his left arm. Another of the shots struck his boot heel, loosing it from the sole of his boot. The shot staggered him, causing him to fall.

The missing boot heel may have also saved Cam from catching a bullet. He tumbled uncontrollably, crashing to the ground below.

Seeing Aiden's killer getting away, Slate struggled to push his way through the crowd. It was useless. Realizing he could do nothing to stop the man, Callfield let out a harsh string of profanities, no longer caring who might be around to hear them.

Ellis landed on the opposite side of the train yard, safely away from the guns trying to take his life. His body struck the ground with a dull thud. Quickly coming to his senses, and knowing he had to escape, Cam managed to get to his feet. Hobbling, running and limping, he approached a man who was leading his horse.

"I need your horse right now," he shouted, pulling the gun from his holster.

The man's protests were immediately cut short by a blast from Cam's six-gun, leaving a smoking, bloody hole in the stranger's shirt. As the man collapsed in the street, a woman shrieked at the sight of the man's murder.

Ellis threw himself in the saddle, slapping the spurs to his mount.

Moments later, the horse was stretched out in a full gallop, the tail flying in the wind behind them. Cameron Ellis was racing westward, away from the shooting, away from the danger, away from Cheyenne.

Chapter Fifteen

While most of the crowd had scattered from the shooting at the train depot, Slate Callfield knelt beside the lone gunshot victim, the one whose horse had been stolen. It was too late to do anything to help him. The man was dead.

Slate motioned to some of the townspeople to take the man's body to the undertaker. Despite the fact that Callfield had no jurisdiction in Cheyenne, he was currently the only lawman on the scene. The men simply responded to the badge he wore.

Grabbing the victim by his arms and legs, a pair of men carried him away. But their actions did nothing to hide the stains that marked an innocent soul's passing.

Still kneeling where the body had fallen, Slate began to study the tracks. He wanted to remember them. For as soon as he acquired another horse, he planned to be off on the man's trail once again.

"Don't move a muscle, son," Clements said, holding a cocked six-gun against the back of his neck, "and you might live out the day. Now, stand up!"

As Callfield slowly turned around to face the man, he could see the gun was leveled on his mid-section. The face was unfamiliar to him, but the man's description wasn't.

Nobody could have missed the prominent, skull-shaped scar on the man's face. Slate knew the man's name. This had to be Skull Clements.

"I would have killed you back there," Clements said, "if your horse hadn't stuck his head in the way."

"So, you're the knobhead who killed my mount," Slate grumbled. "If you care to holster that gun for a couple of minutes, I'll take the price of him out of your mangy hide!"

"After I get you back to the jail," Joe said. "I might just give you the chance." Suddenly, Clements saw the badge on his shirt. "You're a lawman?"

"Yeah, I'm a lawman!" Slate blustered. "You didn't think I was shooting that Sharps at the President did you?"

Clements had always been a good one at reading the faces of others. There was a simple honesty in the young man's eye, a quality that instantly rang true with the famed gunman.

"I guess maybe I did," Joe replied, before holstering his gun. "Sorry about your horse."

"I'm a lot more upset about the man who just got away," Slate muttered, now brushing the dirt from his clothes.

"Man, I'm glad to see you're all right, kid!" Gain said, wrapping his arms around Slate in a big bear hug. "Thought you were dead there for a minute."

"You know this man?" Joe asked.

"Yes, I know him," Gain replied. "This is Slate Callfield, the miserable, thieving young man who stole away my only daughter."

"That would make him your son-in-law."

"Don't ever let anybody tell you that gunmen ain't smart," Gain whispered softly, before elbowing Slate in the ribs. "I see you've already met my friend, Joe Clements, the skull-faced horse killer from Arizona."

"Pleased to meet you, Joe" he said, offering his hand.

"Same here, Slate," Clements muttered, before turning a hard eye on the aged gunman. "Why didn't you say something, Gain? I could have killed him."

"The whole thing happened so fast, I didn't have time to say anything," Carson explained, immediately sensing the fear in his friend's face. Then he put a firm hand on Clements's shoulder. "It scared me too, Joe."

"Is Cleveland okay?" Slate said.

"He's fine," Gain replied.

"That's good."

Suddenly, Callfield saw something that caught his attention. Over next to the building, where the sniper had just been, he saw the weapon.

Bewildered, Gain and Joe simply looked at each other. Slate said nothing as he moved in that direction. The two men simply followed.

As Slate stooped down to pick up something from the ground, they saw the object that had demanded the young man's attention.

Lying there, covered in dirt, was Aiden Frye's rifle.

The slug from Callfield's Sharps had left its mark on the telescopic sight, destroying it for any future use. Other than the scope, the weapon was unharmed.

"Look at that, Gain," Joe said, pointing at the damage. "Now I know why the man missed. Your boy here got a piece of his rifle."

"I should have gotten him," he muttered, bitterly.

"You would have," Gain offered, "if not for the horse killer."

Clements shot the old man an evil stare, which was quickly met by a smile and a wink.

"You recognize this gun?" Slate asked.

Silently, Gain stared at the weapon. "Now that you mention it, it kind of reminds me of Aiden Frye's weapon."

"It *is* his rifle," Slate replied. "Or it was."

"Aiden's dead?"

"It happened a couple of days ago. Frye was on his way back home," Slate explained, "when he stopped to make camp for the night. Best Jerry and I could tell, somebody hailed his campfire. Gain, the man was afoot. After the stranger ate Frye's food and drank his coffee, he ran an old branding iron through the deputy's heart.

"I've been tracking the man ever since," he continued, pointing to the rooftop. "Aiden Frye's killer was your sniper, the man who tried to kill the president."

"Are you sure it was the same guy?" Clements said.

"I'm sure, Joe."

"And now he's gotten away again," Gain said, bitterly.

Since all of the shooting had died down, some of the townspeople began to return to the train depot. A few of the more hardy ones never left. As the minutes passed, more and more of them began to return.

Despite Langston's pleas that the president should remain inside the safety of the train, Cleveland insisted that he would go outside and finish his speech. The Commander-in-Chief said that he wouldn't let an assassin's bullet keep him from his duty.

"Office holders are the agents of the people, not their masters," Cleveland declared, boldly. "The presidency is preeminently the people's office."

Although he also shared Langston's concerns for the man's safety, Malone was taken with the president's deep, inner resolve and his remarkable sense of courage. Kell couldn't bring himself to dissuade Cleveland from this brave decision.

Jeremiah was furious. And proud.

Flanked by Kellen Malone, Denton Turner, and Jeremiah Langston, President Cleveland returned to the railing of the caboose. Behaving as if nothing had ever happened, the president began shaking the hands of the assembled well-wishers.

A number of returning members of the brass band started playing the music they had practiced so faithfully for the past week. Upon hearing the music, the townspeople grudgingly started to filter back to the train depot.

The citizens of Cheyenne were a resilient people, Americans who carved a great city out of a vast, untamed wilderness. These brave souls, who hadn't given way to floods, famine, drought, Indian attacks, locusts, tornadoes, hardship, or the brutal slaughter of a nation at war, wouldn't let a few bullets keep them away.

After everything that had just happened, they figured if the president was bold enough to dare speaking to them once again, then they were certainly brave enough to hear whatever the man had to say.

Once again taking his place behind the lectern, President Cleveland cleared his throat and began to speak. For a time, none of the three said anything. Gain, Joe, and Slaton were content to listen to the words the man chose to deliver.

"A government for the people," Cleveland began, "must depend for its success on the intelligence, the morality, the justice, and the interest of the people themselves."

"Now there's a man!" Clements declared.

"Right you are," Gain added. "So what are you going to do now, Slate?"

"As soon as I get a horse, I'm going after Cam."

"What did you just say?" Clements said.

"I said that I was going after him."

"The name, I mean," Clements replied. "What did you call him?"

"The man at the general store called him Cam," Slate explained. "I don't know his last name." Callfield turned his gaze from one to the other. "Does that name mean anything to you, Gain?"

"It may," Gain said. "Cameron Ellis tried to kill the president when we were headed this way on the train. After the attempt, Kellen Malone threw him over the rail."

"Off the train," Slate said, scratching his head. "Now that would explain what Jerry told me. He backtrailed Aiden's killer and told me that the man had been tossed from the train. It has to be the same guy."

In just a few moments, Clements briefly described Cameron Ellis to the young marshal, since Slaton had been the man who got the best glimpse of the sniper. Upon hearing Cam's description, Slate affirmed that it sounded like the killer he was chasing. Joe's description of the man also seemed to match what the man at the general store said about Cam, as well.

Cameron Ellis," he muttered, "isn't he some kind of a shootist?"

"A stone cold killer," Joe said.

Slate kind of smiled. "I heard the same thing about you."

"Yeah," Clements stated, "but those reports are all true."

"Threw him off the train, huh? I'd like to meet the man who had enough grit to do that."

"Why don't you?" Gain said. "He's right over there, on the president's train."

"I don't have time," Slate said. "I have a killer to catch."

"I've got a better idea," Gain declared. "Why not let the killer come to you?"

"Gain, you've got a pretty good head on your shoulders," Clements said, with a smile, "for an old man." Clements looked over at the bewildered Callfield. "Ellis has already made two attempts on the president's life. Gain, here, thinks Cam isn't done."

"I get it," Slate replied. "You're telling me that you think Cam will try again?"

"Yes, I do," Gain replied.

"If you go with us," Joe explained. "Then Ellis will probably come to you."

"Unless, of course, you really like long horse rides," Gain offered.

"And then I'll kill him or see him hang," Slate muttered. "It's up to him."

"But you may have to wait in line behind somebody else," Joe stated, casting an eye in Carson's direction. "Malone will probably kill him on sight."

"Come on, Joe. Let's go see Kell. He's going to love the story you've got to tell," Gain stated, throwing an arm around Slate's shoulder, as he started walking towards the train. "Tell me, son. Have you ever considered the benefits of rail transportation, the chance to travel clear across the country in days, instead of months?"

Clements looked over at Slaton. "Is he like this all the time?"

"No," Slate replied. "Sometimes he's worse."

"Glad he ain't my father-in-law," Joe muttered.

Chapter Sixteen

As most of the Denver townspeople were sleeping, Billy was hard at work on his nightly duties at the saloon. Five nights a week, he would go there, generating just enough money to meet the young man's meager needs.

The whisky glasses and beer mugs had been cleaned, dried, and placed back underneath the bar. The chairs and tables had been wiped down. Then he emptied and cleaned all of the spittoons, a thankless job, that most people would have despised.

Billy was just happy and grateful for the work.

With all of chairs upside down on the tables, the young man was nearly at the end of his shift. After he finished brushing the last of the floor sweepings out into the street, Billy walked back into the saloon.

About that time, a couple of men entered the door behind him.

Kansas Jack and Avery Sims were a couple of hired guns who worked for Vincent Fielding. Both of them were clean and neat in appearance.

Both of them were capable men with a gun. However, they each preferred another method of killing.

Kansas Jack was an unrepentant brawler, a man who had killed at least three men with his bare hands, in saloon brawls or in bare-knuckle exhibitions. His nose was large and misshapen from the punishment he had suffered; his opponents generally looked much worse.

Although Avery Sims took great pride in the things he could do with a gun, it never gave him quite the same measure of satisfaction as the men he killed with a knife.

Sims always believed that anybody could pull a trigger. A gun was too clinical and impersonal. It was almost cowardly. In addition, a gun offered the user a means to kill from a safe distance.

But Avery didn't see himself as a killer, but rather a technician.

Killing somebody with a knife was a deeply personal exercise. It allowed him an opportunity to look the victim in the eye. It also made it possible for Sims to deliver an effective message from the one who hired him, letting the victim fully understand the circumstances that led to his death.

Most of all, a knife offered Avery the most individual gratification, the chance for him to closely witness the soul leaving the body. He truly lived for that one special moment.

"Good evening, Billy?" said Jack.

Good evening to you too, Kansas," Billy said, with a look of bewilderment. "I'm sorry. But the saloon is closed. You'll have to come back tomorrow."

"We're not here for a drink," Avery said. "Vincent Fielding sent us."

"Well," Billy said, "it's closed for him too."

"Are you trying to be funny, dummy?"

"No, Avery," Billy replied. "Just trying to be helpful. And please don't call me dummy."

"You shouldn't have hurt Mr. Fielding today," Kansas explained. "He wanted us to teach you a lesson."

"I love lessons," Billy said, still holding the broom. "The McGuffey Readers are my favorites."

"I think I'm going to love cutting his kid," Avery declared, moving the blade back and forth, in an intimidating manner.

"Leave him alone," Kansas said. "He's just a little slow. And Fielding doesn't want him dead, just hurt."

"Then maybe Fielding should've done it for himself."

"Shut up, Avery!" Kansas blustered. "What I'm trying to tell you, Billy, is that Fielding didn't like it when you hurt him."

"Then he shouldn't have hurt Miss Jenny."

"Let me explain it to him, Kansas," Avery said. "Fielding wants us to hurt you, too."

Although Billy didn't fully comprehend their reason for being here, he did understand that Vincent was angry with him. He also knew that Sims was a bad man, somebody who liked to hurt people with a knife.

"I don't think I would like that," Billy stated.

"I've listened to enough stupid talk," Avery said. "Now I'm going to hurt the boy."

Forgetting all about the orders to just hurt the young man, Sims charged at Billy, trying to plant the blade deep within his ribs. Billy quickly stepped aside, letting Sims go right on past him. Then he grabbed Sims from behind, running the broomstick under Avery's chin. Holding the stick on each side of the man's jaw, he lifted the man off the ground.

Sims, still clinging to the knife, was helpless to do anything with it. He struggled to breathe. He fought to get loose. As the loss of oxygen was causing him to grow dizzy, Sims desperately tried to break free. The blade fell from his fingers.

"You shouldn't call me stupid," Billy said, continuing to hold Sims aloft.

Fearful that Billy would kill Avery, but unsure of what he should do, Jack picked up a chair and smashed it over Billy's shoulders. The blow caused the young man to drop the unconscious Sims to the saloon floor.

"That wasn't nice of you, Jack," Billy said, turning to face Kansas Jack.

Jack threw a couple of blows to the young man's belly, punches that would have downed a lesser man. Then he threw a hard right towards Billy's jaw, a blow that the young man caught on his forearm.

A man not accustomed to losing fights, Kansas Jack's eyes grew large with fear.

Billy backhanded Jack across the face, sending the brawler across the upturned chairs on a saloon table. Jack's unconscious body crashed to the floor. The man finally got his knees under him. He tried to rise. Then, he collapsed to the floor in a heap.

Outside, the sheriff's deputy, Len Cagle, was making his nightly rounds through the town. Upon hearing heard the commotion, Cagle had chosen to investigate the noise coming from the saloon.

Unknown to Billy, the deputy had seen the final blows of the fight.

"Are you okay, Billy?"

"Yes," Billy replied, momentarily fearful of the unexpected voice behind him. "They tried to hurt me."

"I could see that."

"I'm sorry about the mess," Billy said, holding out his hands so the deputy could put the cuffs on him.

Cagle laughed. "I'm not going to arrest you, Billy."

"You're not going to arrest me? But I made a mess."

"I'll make you a deal, Billy," Cagle said, soberly. "If you help me get these two over to the jail, then I'll think about letting you go. But you have to promise to come back over here, Billy, and clean up the mess."

"I promise," Billy replied. "You'll be real happy with the job I'll do."

"I'm sure I will be," the deputy said, with a smile. "Now, let's get these two over to the jail. It'll be a good place for them to sleep it off."

The young man easily lifted the unconscious men, putting one of them under each arm. The deputy's jaw dropped. Figuring that Billy would assist him in carrying their bodies, Cagle was astounded by the display of strength. Without so much as a groan, Billy started towards the jail with the men.

"You want me to help you?"

"No, Deputy. I've got them," Billy said. "They called me stupid."

"Well, they probably won't do that anymore."

***

"That's the whole story," Joseph Blakemore said.

Despite his discomfort with hearing the details of the conspiracy, Blakemore's attorney silently listened to the story. He sipped his coffee. Patrick Alexander had been his attorney for many years. His face showed neither condemnation, nor approval.

"Do you have any idea what you've done?" Alexander said.

"Yes, I do."

"I don't think you do, Joseph. This is extremely serious," he added. "Although I am bound by my oath to keep your involvement private, I wish I had never learned about it. I also find it hard to believe that you allowed yourself to become a party to it.

"What were you thinking? This wasn't even a simple murder, if there is such a thing. This was a conspiracy, an attempt on a president's life. You'll be lucky if you don't hang."

"I suppose that's your job, to keep me off the gallows."

"Despite my skills as a barrister, I'm not sure if even I can accomplish that, especially if the president dies. Our great nation has scarcely recovered from Lincoln's assassination. This will only serve to stoke those bitter and dreadful embers once again."

"What do you think I should do, Patrick?"

"As an officer of the court, I urge you to confess your involvement in this plot. Perhaps you can spare yourself a hangman's rope."

"But what if I testified against Vincent Fielding and Wilson Stonegate?

"I have no doubt that your immediate cooperation would significantly help your case," Patrick replied. "And it might keep your wife from becoming a widow."

"Then you can count on me to do it."

"Very well," Patrick said.

"They still have one more attack on the president planned."

"Are you sure?"

"Yes, Patrick. Wilson told me all about it." Blakemore walked to the window, staring out at the California city of Sacramento. "I no longer can be a part of it!"

"Does Karen know?

"No, I have said nothing to her about it."

"I will go make the necessary arrangements," Alexander stated. "Meanwhile, you need to break this news to your wife, Joseph. Please don't let her read about it in the newspaper."

Blakemore hung his head at the thought. Grimly, he realized that the news would be devastating to the woman. Her shame and embarrassment, Joseph feared those things more than a prison sentence. He was also concerned what the knowledge would do to his children.

The taunts of schoolchildren can often be vicious to their fellow classmates. Joseph could only speculate how much more cruel it would be for his son and daughter, when the children of the less affluent families in their school learned of his crimes.

"Patrick, before you go," Blakemore said, "I want you to take this letter. I have recorded every minute detail of our arrangement. If anything should happen to me, I want you to take this to the authorities. Will you do that?"

"Sure, I will."

"I need you to promise."

Okay, Joseph. You have my word," Alexander said, stuffing the envelope into the breast pocket of his coat. "But what makes you think your life might be in danger?"

"You're much too bright a man, Patrick, to be so foolish. Vincent Fielding is an animal, a cruel man who exhibits no conscience or remorse. He once had a man killed for simply insulting him. And Wilson Stonegate isn't much better.

"In addition, these are men who conspired to kill a president. Do you think that they would hesitate to kill anyone who they perceived to be a threat to their plans?"

"I understand. But nobody is privy to the particulars of this conversation, Joseph. Besides, it *is* public knowledge that I am your lawyer," Alexander explained. "Why would anybody have any reason to suspect that this was anything more than just a routine, weekly meeting with your attorney?"

"I suppose I am just being paranoid."

"I think so," Patrick offered, pausing in the doorway. "You remember what the Scriptures say about that, don't you?"

"What's that?"

"The wicked flee when no man pursueth."

"Are you saying I'm wicked?" Joseph said.

"No, I'm not. Only you and the Lord can sufficiently answer that question," Patrick explained. "I will say that conspiring to kill a president generally places a person in the company of the wicked.

"Please don't continue to trouble yourself about this matter, Joseph. I am confident that we can come to some suitable resolution Most important of all, you must talk to Karen. Do it now! I shall see you later."

When the door closed behind the attorney, Blakemore pulled open the upper desk drawer on his desk. He momentarily considered using the gun that he saw there. Joseph finally settled on the bottle that was in the lower drawer.

From just down the street, Wilson Stonegate watched the lawyer leaving Blakemore's office. Stonegate checked his watch. The two of them had been in there for a long time.

When the lawyer saw Stonegate watching him, he briefly nodded.

Wilson returned the gesture.

For quite some time now, Vincent Fielding had commented to him that Blakemore's uncertainty left him feeling uneasy.

Recently, Wilson had begun to share those same feelings.

Chapter Seventeen

As President and Mrs. Cleveland were enjoying a few peaceful moments alone in his room, Jeremiah Langston brought in a document he had just received.

"I apologize for bothering the two of you. And good evening to you, Frances. Here is the report you've waiting for from the Land Office agents, sir."

"It's about time," he said.

"If you will excuse me, Mr. Langston," Frances said, starting towards the door, "I will leave you two alone. Please feel free to discuss your business, while I go freshen up."

"Thank you, ma'am," Langston replied.

"Please make sure that Captain Turner or Mr. Malone knows your whereabouts, dear," Cleveland said. "We cannot be certain that all of the danger has passed."

"As you wish, Grover," Frances said, smiling sweetly as she left the room.

President Cleveland folded his newspaper and set it aside, before taking the report from Langston. "Thank you, Jeremiah. Was the problem as bad as we suspected?"

The document contained a detailed list of the individuals who had been discovered to have obtained government land through questionable means. It also described how those individuals were selfishly using the land to enrich themselves. In addition, the report documented how the land's current use bore no resemblance to the original terms of its acquisition.

"No, Mr. President. It was worse, much worse."

Cleveland briefly scanned the report, catching the key headlines and details, before turning his attention to the names on the list.

"I want to give this report a lot more careful study before we reach Sacramento," the president stated. "But I would assume that one of the names on this list stood out for you. Am I correct, Jeremiah?"

"You mean Vincent Fielding?"

"Yes, that's the one," the president said.

"It has to be more than a coincidence," Langston declared. "The threats, the attempts on your life, sir—his name just keeps popping up. Fielding even tried to hire Joe Clements to kill Kellen Malone, the man directly in charge of your security. Common sense would dictate that there has to be some kind of a connection."

"I must admit that I was skeptical," Cleveland said. "At first I thought you were jumping to conclusions. Perhaps I owe you an apology, Jeremiah."

"I understand, Mr. President," Langston said. "What do you want to do about the man?"

Cleveland lowered his gaze, staring at his assistant over top of his reading spectacles. "I think we should send some troops to San Francisco and have Fielding detained for questioning."

"When do you want to do this?"

"Immediately!"

"I will notify Captain Turner of your instructions," Langston said. "I think we also need to determine the names and locations of his closest associates, Mr. President. If we are correct about Fielding, it might also be a good idea to investigate those with whom he routinely does business."

"I'm definitely going to trust your instincts on this one," Cleveland stated. "That sounds prudent to me, as well. If there is no connection between Mr. Fielding's business partners and this conspiracy, then we will know for certain.

"I have to admit, Jeremiah, I am a little uncomfortable with the actions that this situation has forced me to take," the president added, briefly staring into space as he gathered his thoughts. "Inherently, I believe this office is a uniquely sacred American institution."

"Then doesn't that make it worth protecting?" Langston asked.

"Of course it does," Cleveland said. "When Booth killed Abraham Lincoln, he didn't just kill a president; he attacked the principles and virtues upon which our great country was founded. However, those lofty ideals seemed to hold more sway with me, when I wasn't the person occupying this noble office."

"Our only responsibility is to preserve the structure," Langston said, "not to measure ourselves against the architect."

Cleveland nodded appreciatively.

Then Langston's thoughts returned to the land Office report. "By the way, Mr. President, what do you plan to do about these fraudulent land acquisitions?"

"This report does nothing other than identifying a number of the guilty parties," Cleveland said, removing his spectacles, "and how they failed to carry out their obligations. I have already given this matter a great deal of thought. My mind is made up.

"There has been a great abuse of the public trust, Jeremiah. I will not allow it to go unpunished," the president added, waving his spectacles to emphasize the point. "Before I leave Sacramento, I will issue an executive order to return those lands to the public domain. In addition, we will take court action against those offenders, whose speculative interests were harmful to meager settlers, just trying to make a better life for themselves and their families."

Jeremiah nodded.

"Okay, sir. If there is nothing else you need from me tonight," Langston said, moving towards the door. "We have an early day awaiting us tomorrow in Sacramento. I think I will turn in for the night."

"No, I think that is all, Jeremiah. Get some sleep. You've earned it."

"By the way, I am certain," Langston said, "that Lincoln would approve of your efforts as president, sir."

"Need I remind you, Jeremiah?" the president said. "If Mr. Lincoln would approve of my efforts, I might do well to stay away from the theater."

***

A warm, peaceful Sacramento evening was softly overtaken by the darkness. Most of the city's businessmen had left for the day, going home to their wives and families, leaving another group of individuals, less savory ones, in charge of the city's nightlife.

Under any other circumstances, Joseph Blakemore's day would have already ended. He would normally be home now, eating dinner and spending time with his loved one.

Filled with guilt and self-doubt, the businessman had just downed his third shot of whiskey when a knock sounded on the door. It was only the calming effects of the liquor that kept him from being startled.

He quickly scrawled his signature on the paper in front of him, folded it, and placed it under where the whiskey bottle was kept. Strangely enough, that was always the place where he left his love notes to Karen.

She always looked for them there.

"Come on in," Blakemore said.

Joseph's heart was immediately gripped with fear, upon seeing Wilson Stonegate enter the room. Then he thought about the Scripture that Patrick had shared with him.

The wicked flee when no man pursueth.

Perhaps he *was* being paranoid. Alexander was right; there was nothing suspicious about a businessman regularly meeting with his attorney.

"So, I see you're drinking alone," Stonegate said. "I've been told that drinking alone is the sign of a drunkard."

"I've been told that drinking alone is a good indication that a man has no friends to drink with," Joseph said, wryly. "Care for some?"

"I don't think so. But thanks," Wilson said. "What do you mean you have no friends to drink with? Vincent and I have been here for you all along."

"I know that, Wilson. It was just a joke. That's all."

"I have to tell you, Joseph, from the very beginning, Vincent has often questioned your loyalties."

"My loyalties?"

"Yes, Joseph, your loyalties to us and to our plan," Stonegate explained. "But I have always been there for you, to assure Vincent that you were a man who could be trusted."

"Thank you, Wilson."

"Don't be so quick to thank me, Joseph. The past few days, I have begun to question your loyalties, as well."

As he sat listening to Wilson, Blakemore's arms were crossed in front of his chest. He gently uncrossed them, placing them on the arms of his chair. Momentarily, his eyes shifted from Wilson to his upper desk drawer.

"What are you saying?"

"I am saying that I now agree with Vincent. Perhaps he was right about you, after all."

Blakemore laughed without humor.

"And all this time, I thought I was the one who was being paranoid," Joseph replied, slowly inching his hand towards the desk drawer. "I've done absolutely nothing to betray you."

"You're lying, Joseph! You and I both know it."

Blakemore said nothing as he gently eased open the desk drawer. Perhaps the whiskey had calmed his nerves, for his face showed none of the fear he was feeling.

"What did you tell Patrick Alexander?"

"So you're spying on me now?" Joseph said.

"Do I need to?"

"Alexander is my attorney," he said. "You know I meet with him every week."

Blakemore now had the drawer open far enough to see the item he was seeking. Ever so slowly, he inched his hand towards the gun.

"I guess I would be more likely to believe you," Stonegate said, "if you weren't concentrating so hard on what you have in that desk drawer."

At those words, Blakemore froze. Then he saw the two-shot derringer that Stonegate had produced from his coat.

"Now, what do you think I should do about you, Joseph?"

"How about letting me go about my own business?"

"Humor, in the face of death, I like that quality in a man," Stonegate said. "I never figured you for courage."

"Maybe it isn't courage, after all. It might just be the liquor talking."

Blakemore continued to look for an opening, a distraction, something that might give him a chance to pick up the gun. His eyes were constantly moving, back and forth, from Stonegate to the desk drawer.

"And now I see humility, too," Stonegate declared. "It almost pains me to kill a man of your depth."

"You don't want to kill me, Wilson."

"Why not?"

"Because, if you kill me, you will hang," Blakemore explained, still considering the prospects of reaching for the gun. "I gave a letter to my attorney that outlines every facet of your involvement in this plot. It also mentions Vincent's role in the conspiracy. If anything were to happen to me, I gave Patrick explicit instructions to take that letter to the authorities."

Still holding the derringer on Blakemore, Stonegate reached into his breast pocket with his left hand. "You mean this letter?"

"Why that damned turncoat!" Joseph muttered, bitterly. "My own lawyer was working for you all along."

"The tentacles of Vincent Fielding are everywhere," Stonegate said, with cruel laughter. "If it helps any, Alexander was pleased that you hadn't yet spoken with Karen. Neither of us had any real interest in the murder of a woman."

"You're all heart, Wilson."

"There's that remarkable sense of humor again," Stonegate said, feigning a look of admiration. "I am going to have to go now, before anyone shows up. You have any last words?"

"None that you'd care to repeat to anyone."

"I do like you, Joseph," he added. "You can go to your grave knowing that your wife will be well-cared for. Vincent Fielding has often commented to me that Karen knew how to fill out a skirt. He thought that maybe she needed a man like him."

As much as the talk about Karen outraged him, Blakemore refused to let the comments goad him into a fight before he was ready.

"How about one last drink?" Blakemore said. "One for the road."

"Go ahead, Joseph. You'll understand if I don't join you."

Blakemore poured himself one more shot of whiskey. And despite his desire for a momentary distraction, Stonegate's attention on his prey had never wavered. He knew there would be no other chance.

Blakemore was also under no illusions that he was particularly skilled with a gun. But he knew there would be no other chances. Also, Blakemore feared that Karen might suddenly come to his office. He knew Stonegate would have no reservations about killing her, if that was what it required to keep his actions secret.

The time was now.

Blakemore lifted his glass in mocking salute. "Here's to you and Vincent! May you two get everything in this life that you have coming."

Just as Blakemore put the glass to his lips, he dropped it.

Instinctively, Stonegate's eyes were drawn to the dropped liquor glass. Seizing the moment, Blakemore grasped the gun and brought it level. He almost made it.

Just then, a bullet burned a hole though his insides, knocking him back into his chair.

Fearing that he would be discovered, Stonegate resisted the urge to put another bullet into the man. Wilson opened the door, checked both ways, and then ran for the cover of the shadows.

Once the short, balding man was safely obscured in the darkness, he stopped to catch his breath. Stonegate was sure that nobody saw him leave Blakemore's office.

As the man sat there in his chair dying, Blakemore was glad that he had been paranoid. The letter he left for Karen told the whole story. It begged her forgiveness. It also spoke of his love for her.

Sadly, he realized that it said nothing of Patrick Alexander's involvement. Moreover, he feared that Karen would find his letter and take it to his attorney for advice.

Mortally wounded, the man knew he only had a few minutes to live. Using his own blood for ink, his finger for a pen, and his desk for parchment, Blakemore quickly wrote four simple words to those who would find his body.

Satisfied with what he had done, Blakemore's final thoughts were of his wife and children. Perhaps this was best. Maybe his family would be spared the embarrassment of his involvement in this scandal.

Blakemore's lips turned up in a smile. His head slumped back against his chair.

Then he was still.

Chapter Eighteen

After Cameron Ellis' attack on the president at the Cheyenne train depot, the rest of the trip had been without incident. Still, Kellen Malone and the rest of Cleveland's bodyguards hadn't relaxed.

There had already been several attempts on the president's life. Kellen Malone was much too wise to doubt that the conspirators had given up on their plans.

It was about an hour before dawn. With the train about forty miles east of Sacramento, the engineer suddenly began to slow the locomotive to a stop.

There were a couple of huge bonfires, blazing away on each side of the track. In between those fires, the railroad track was littered with railroad ties and brush. As much as he hated to stop, the engineer was fearful of trying to run the blockade.

Captain Turner sprinted towards the president's room, where he was met in the doorway by Kellen Malone. Moments later, the pair of them were joined by Joe Clements, Gain Carson, and Slate Callfield.

"Why is the train stopping?" Turner said.

"I don't know," Malone replied.

"It could be another attack."

"I thought the same thing," Malone said. "I want you to send about six of your men to the front of the train to see what's going on."

"I've already done that," he said. "I gave them clear instructions to get the train moving."

"Is that all you told them?" Kell asked.

"No, it wasn't, sir. I told them to shoot anyone who tries to stop them."

"Good," Malone added. "Send another half dozen to the caboose. Don't expose them to gunfire; keep them inside. We'll stay with the president, here in this car."

"Okay, Malone. Be careful."

"Same to you, Dent."

As soon as Turner rushed off to rally his soldiers, Malone sprang into action. "Let's go, sir," he shouted. "We don't have much time."

The president threw back the covers, revealing that he was already fully dressed.

"I'm ready when you are, Kell," Cleveland declared.

"Will you two be okay here?" Malone said to Joe and Gain.

"We'll be fine, Malone" Joe said. "So will the women."

"I'm counting on it."

"They'll be safe as they were in their mothers' arms," Carson added.

"Okay. See you boys in Sacramento," Kell said, catching up the shotgun behind the door. Then he slightly opened the door to check on the progress of Turner and his blue-clad soldiers. "Come on, Slate! Time's wasting."

With the soldiers headed off to their station in the caboose, Malone led the way. Following closely behind him was the president and Slate Callfield.

In the dim light of the moon, three dark figures climbed down from the train. Behind them came the unmistakable sound of a rifle, levering a round into the chamber. The sound was loud and clear, in the gentle stillness of the night.

"Where do you think you're going, Malone?" Turner said.

"Figured this might be safer than taking the train into Sacramento," Malone replied. "You and I both know there will be a reception waiting for us there. We might not be able to protect Cleveland the next time."

"Why didn't you tell me your plans in advance?" Turner blustered. "I'm responsible for the president's safety, too."

"Look, Dent," Malone said with a laugh. "I can't be sure who is on this train or who might be watching us. I needed this to be believable. Most of all, I needed it to remain a secret."

"You know I wouldn't tell anybody, sir."

"I never doubted that. I just figured this way was the best," Kell said, squinting to read his watch in the moonlight. "We have to go now, Dent. They'll have those obstacles removed from the tracks in no time."

Turner softly eared back the hammer on his rifle and lowered the gun to his side. He walked up to Malone, soberly staring the man in the eyes. "Based on our past experience, I guess I should have known you would try something like this," he stated, before throwing a hard right hand into Kell's jaw.

Malone never saw it coming.

It was the first undisciplined action that Captain Denton Turner had taken since he first put on the uniform of the United States Army.

Although Malone remained on his feet, the blow from Turner rocked him to his boots. Kell lightly rubbed his jaw, wincing at the pain.

"I will understand, sir," Turner declared, turning his gaze toward the president, "if you feel you have to court martial me, for striking another man while in uniform."

"Court martial you!" Cleveland replied. "Why would I do that, Captain Turner? When Langston discovers what Malone has done here, he will probably insist on giving you a commendation."

In spite of the danger they still faced, all three men laughed at the president's response.

"Joe and Gain know all about our plan," Malone said. "You can't tell anybody else, other than Langston."

"Understood."

"I think you broke my jaw," Malone replied, thrusting out his hand. "By the way, Dent, I'm sorry about keeping this from you."

"No, you're not," Turner said, smiling as he returned the handshake. "And by the way, sir, I hope you're right about the jaw."

With a brief, crisp salute to his Commander-in-Chief, Captain Turner scrambled back aboard the train. Silently, he watched the three men run towards the cover of the woods.

"There's the horses," Malone said. "Right where they're supposed to be."

Upon seeing the three saddled animals, Malone picked up the pace. The president was right on his heels, gamely matching him, step-for-step. Callfield trailed behind the two men, covering their back and watching to see if they'd been discovered.

From the cover of the tree line, Kell watched the soldiers attempting to clear the tracks. Their every movement was brightly illuminated in the light of the two fires. Scarcely ten minutes later, the soldiers were aboard the train and the president's locomotive was steaming on its way to Sacramento.

President Cleveland watched it pull away without him.

Moving quickly, Malone shoved the shotgun into the laces that were holding on his bedroll. Before climbing into the saddle, he made sure the president was safely mounted. As he prepared to mount up, a deep voice from the darkness broke the silence.

"We've been waiting for you, Malone."

***

When the president's train arrived in Sacramento, there was a large crowd waiting outside the train depot. Among the crowd of politicians, citizens, and well-wishers, there were also three other interested parties, waiting for the president to step down from the train.

Realizing that the president was nowhere to be found on the train, Jeremiah Langston was fuming when he finally located Joe Clements.

Clements, Gain Carson, Rachel Malone, and Frances Cleveland were all sharing a nice breakfast in the dining car when he found them.

Upon seeing Langston enter the car, Carson gently elbowed Rachel and nodded his head towards Jeremiah. "You don't want to miss this, ma'am," he said. "It's going to be funny."

Unable to hide her amusement that someone could be as infuriated at her husband as she often was, Rachel laughed softly behind her coffee cup.

Despite his growing sense of anger, Langston pulled up a chair alongside the four diners.

"Good morning, ladies. Same to you, Mr. Carson," he muttered. Then he turned his gaze towards Joe. "Mr. Clements, I have looked all over this train for President Cleveland and Kellen Malone. Can you tell me where they are?"

"They arranged for some different transportation," Joe said.

"Different transportation?" Langston blustered. "What's that mean?"

"It means they got off the train."

"I know what it means," Langston said, deliberately trying to lower his voice, so he wasn't heard by the other passengers. "But where did they go? Come to think of it, where did that young Marshal Callfield go? Was he in on this, too?"

"They're headed to the same place we are, Langston. Sacramento."

"Is there somebody at this table," Langston said, "who can give me a straight answer?"

"About the time you were sleeping comfortably in your bed last night, somebody stopped the train," Carson explained. "Malone and

Callfield snuck the president off the train, when the soldiers were clearing the debris off the tracks."

"Whose stupid idea was that one?"

"It was Mr. Malone's," Frances interrupted, "and my husband's."

"I'm sorry, ma'am," Langston replied. "I didn't mean to imply…"

"Relax, Jeremiah," she said, sweetly. "Everything is fine. I am certain that Grover is in capable hands. That isn't to say that I'm not worried about him. I am. However, Rachel Malone's husband has successfully met every challenge he's faced. And I definitely trust him with the president's life. Now, if you will allow him to finish, Mr. Clements will explain the whole thing to you."

"From day one, Malone never one time intended on riding this train all the way into Sacramento," Joe declared. "It always was a fool's errand. I'll give you three to one odds that they've already got some guns waiting for us outside the train. If the president stepped off this train, not five seconds later, the man would be stone cold dead. Several of us might just die with him. Malone wasn't going to let that happen."

Grudgingly, Langston nodded in agreement.

"You served with Malone in the Army, didn't you, Jeremiah?" Gain asked.

"Yes, I did."

"I'm figuring Kell didn't always follow your commands to the letter. Am I correct?"

"You certainly are," Langston replied. "We often thought of having him court martialed."

"I'm also guessing that he led you out of a couple of enemy traps or ambushes."

"How did you know?"

"I know Kellen Malone," Gain replied. "It's hard to put a soldier on trial who saves your life and gets results on the battlefield."

"Okay! Okay!" Jeremiah said, holding up his hands in surrender. "I also spent enough time in the military to recognize when I am outnumbered." He turned his attention to Joe. "What is Malone's plan now, Mr. Clements?"

"I can't say for sure," Joe said, rubbing his chin. "First, he will get the president safely into town. Then he will get in touch with us."

"Then what happens?"

"Then, Mr. Langston," Joe stated, "all hell will break loose!"

"Now that sounds like the Kellen Malone I remember," Gain said.

"And the one I'm married to," Rachel added.

Chapter Nineteen

When the man spoke to him from the darkness, Kell didn't even bother to turn around. He already knew the voice.

"And don't even think of going for those guns, kid. I'd cut you in half before you turned around," the man from the darkness said, backing up his boast with the promise of his double barreled shot gun.

Although Slate's first impulse had been to grab iron, he waited for Malone to start the ball, or the pair of masked strangers to make some hostile action.

Quietly, President Cleveland sat astride his horse. He knew he had no weapon; he had only to watch, or try to escape if things went sour.

"What do you two men want?" Slate said.

"We're looking for your friend," the stranger replied.

"Well, you found me," Kell said. "Now, what are you going to do about it?"

Bewildered, Callfield then saw the two strangers lower the neckerchiefs that covered the lower halves of their faces. Removing their masks, it was strange behavior for an outlaw. It could only signal just one of two things.

Either the two men planned to leave nobody alive to identify them, or they meant them no real harm. Slate hoped for the latter. In his mind, he was prepared for either result.

The smaller one, the youngster who wasn't talking, started walking quickly towards Malone. He said absolutely nothing. Then he threw his arms around Malone, giving the man a strong embrace.

"How are you doing, Pa?"

"Just fine, Jesse. It's good to see you, son. Everything fine at the ranch?"

"Hasn't been a problem since you took care of those rustlers," Jesse explained. "Sheriff Kimball said he would keep an eye on things while we were gone."

"Sounds good," Malone said, moving over to shake the other man's hand. "Nice to see you, Buck,"

"Same here, Kell."

"Have any trouble getting here?" Malone said.

"No, everything went according to plan."

Kell pointed towards the president and Slaton Callfield. "I want you men to meet President Grover Cleveland, on the left. The guy with the star and the itchy gun hand is Marshal Slate Callfield.

"Gentlemen, these two would-be outlaws are my son, Jesse," he continued, "and his uncle, Buck Halstead."

President Cleveland and the others spent a few moments getting acquainted, exchanging pleasantries, and shaking hands.

"It was kind of risky," Malone said, "stepping out of the darkness with those masks on. You might have gotten yourselves shot."

"Sorry about that, Kell," Buck replied. "But we had to make sure it was you, first. And we had to stay hidden from those soldiers. I guess we built the fires a little too big."

"A little too big?" Kell muttered, sarcastically. "When Sherman burned Atlanta, I doubt it was any brighter than that. Lucky they didn't see us leaving the train."

"So, where are we headed now, Pa?"

"Sacramento," Kell said. "I'd like to send you boys back to the ranch, but it's too dangerous with Cam Ellis still on the loose."

"Cam Ellis?" Buck said. "What's he got to do with this?"

"Let's get mounted up first. I'll tell you on the way."

As the five horses and riders started on their way west to Sacramento, Kell explained every detail of their trip. He related to Buck and Jesse about the attacks on the president, the men who were killed in his defense, and the murder of Deputy Aiden Frye.

Kell removed his hat, checked the sky, and wiped his forehead on his sleeve. Then he returned the hat to his head.

"Mr. President, I don't know about you, sir," Kell stated, "but I'm getting real sick and tired of us being shot at."

"What do you suggest?" Cleveland said.

"I think we should start taking the fight to them, Mr. President. Everything we've done this entire trip has been in response to the assassins," Kell explained. "They've set the time; they've chosen the battlefields. These killers have even dictated the terms of battle.

"Their actions have forced us to simply defend our position. No longer! These men wanted a fight, Mr. President. Now they'll get one!"

"I like the way you think," Callfield said. "But how are we going to do it?"

"I might be able to help with that," President Cleveland said. "My investigation into the abuse of public lands has revealed the name of Vincent Fielding."

"Fielding, huh?" Kell said. "The man's name turns up everywhere."

"That's what I thought, as well," Cleveland replied. "Last night, I instructed Langston to send some troops to Fielding's San Francisco office, and have him detained for questioning. I also ordered him to question a number of the man's closest business associates. That may give us some real clue as to the players in this little drama."

"Okay, sir. I'll wait until we get to Sacramento," Kell muttered. "Then we'll see what Langston has to tell us."

"I'm fine with that," Slate replied. "But if I happen to run into Cam Ellis, you need to know that I'll kill that man on sight."

"You may have to shoot your way around me," Kell said.

"Well let's put away the guns for now. Cameron Ellis will wait," the president said, sporting a wide smile. "I haven't been on horseback for quite some time. Now, I just want to enjoy the trip and the scenery. When we get to Sacramento, I plan to buy you all a round of drinks. And, Jesse, we will find something for you, as well."

"I like the way you think, Mr. President," Buck stated.

"Well, thank you, Mr. Halstead."

"Almost makes me sorry," said Buck, "that I never voted for you."

***

When the president's train arrived in Sacramento, there was a large crowd waiting outside the train depot. Among the crowd of politicians, citizens, and well-wishers, there were also three other interested parties, waiting for the president to step down from the train.

All of them waited to see President Cleveland's face.

A number of Chinese residents also came to watch the festivities. Migrating to America to work on the construction of the railroads, a number of them had permanently settled in Sacramento. None of these immigrants had ever seen a national leader. Excitedly, they chatted among themselves in their native tongue.

Next to the train depot was a newly-assembled gallows, which had been pressed into service the day before, for the execution a drunken gambler.

While engaged in a mindless stupor, brought about by a mixture of whisky and opium, the man had killed two prostitutes and the proprietor of the local saloon. Not only had he interrupted the exercise of free trade in the California city, the man's actions also closed the saloon for an hour.

The townspeople hanged him yesterday.

Frugality demanded that Sacramento shouldn't let such a fine structure go to waste.

The mayor, during last night's town meeting, suggested that the gallows would also make an excellent platform for President Cleveland's visit. The assembly soon erupted into laughter and the mayor was humiliated, when a lone voice from the crowd shouted, "Whose job is it to bring the rope?"

Many of those in the crowd, a substantial number of the early arrivals, were already standing around the base of the gallows. The mayor, who had spent hours preparing his speech, waited at the top of the platform for the president's arrival. It was to have been his finest moment in politics.

The blue-clad soldiers were the first ones to step down from the train. Gain Carson was the next to exit, followed closely by Rachel Malone and Frances Cleveland. They pushed their way through the crowd, headed towards the safety of the hotel. Following closely behind them was Joe Clements, covering their flank from any danger.

Jeremiah Langston was the next figure to disembark from the train.

"Ladies and gentlemen," he said, raising his voice to be heard above the crowd. "I regret to inform you that President Cleveland's appearance has been delayed. He should be arriving in Sacramento by tomorrow. We will have more details for you then."

Disappointed by Langston's announcement, many of those in the crowd began to return to their homes, jobs, and activities.

The three armed men, intent on their mission, pushed their way through the mob. As they climbed aboard the train, the conductor asked to see their tickets. Bitterly, they shoved the man aside, a trio of armed men, frightening the passengers, making their way from car to car.

A few minutes later, the three learned that Langston's announcement had been correct. The president wasn't aboard the train. And Stonegate wouldn't be happy.

As the crowd began to disperse, Patrick Alexander also started back towards his office. Like many of the others, the lawyer had come to see the president. However, his reasons for the visit were different than most of those in the crowd.

Alexander expected to witness an assassination.

Unsure of the circumstances that altered President Cleveland's visit, Alexander remembered his activities the night before, the betrayal of Joseph Blakemore. His mind was lost in thought. Suddenly, the lawyer was startled by a voice behind him, someone calling his name.

"Attorney Alexander," the man said.

Turning around to face the man, Patrick saw Sheriff Taylor and a pair of deputies. The lawyer was confident that they had just discovered Blakemore's body. It was understandable that they would come to the man's attorney, to learn something about Blakemore's business interests, and who might have a motive to kill him.

"Sorry to trouble you, Mr. Alexander," the sheriff said. "But would you mind coming with us?"

"Not at all," Patrick replied, smugly. "But it would be beneficial if you would tell me how I might help you."

"We discovered Joseph Blakemore's body a few minutes ago. He's been murdered, shot to death in his office."

"His poor wife, Karen!" Alexander said, feigning a look of shock and sadness. "I just saw my client last evening."

"Then you *do* admit seeing the man before his murder?"

"Now wait just a minute!" the lawyer blustered. "What are you try-ing to say?"

168

As Sheriff Taylor and the deputies stopped to question the man, the crowd leaving Cleveland's postponed appearance began gathering around the men. The deputies made several efforts to disperse the crowd, but to no avail.

The onlookers sensed that, perhaps there was another show to be seen this morning, in the sheriff's conversation with Alexander.

"Mr. Patrick Alexander," Taylor declared, "I am hereby arresting you for the cold-blooded murder of Joseph Blakemore."

The crowd began to buzz at the pronouncement.

Without any further instruction, one of the deputies pulled his revolver, while the other slapped the handcuffs on the wrists of the attorney. Patrick briefly struggled with the men before finally submitting to his arrest.

"What makes you think I killed the man?"

"You admitted that you were the last person to see him alive last night. In fact, Wilson Stonegate confirmed that he saw you enter the man's office before the time of his death."

"That doesn't mean I killed him!"

"Unfortunately for you, Mr. Alexander," the sheriff said, "his was not the only testimony we have against you."

"Listen to me, Sheriff." At the mention of Wilson Stonegate, the lawyer was now frantic. "I'm telling you that I never killed the man!"

"That isn't what the law thinks."

"As an officer of the court, I have a right to know what evidence you have against me."

"Yes, you do, Mr. Alexander. The best testimony we had came from the victim, himself."

As the sheriff and the attorney continued to carry on their conversation, the crowd became larger and larger. The deputies attempted to clear a path, but found it was useless. The mob around them continued to grow.

Alexander was bewildered by the sheriff's statement. "I demand that you tell me what you are talking about, Sheriff Taylor!"

Taylor smiled before continuing. "Before Mr. Blakemore died, he left a message in his own blood. As he died, the man wrote four words: *My lawyer killed me.* The victim's wife, Karen Blakemore, even verified his writing for us."

Although the attorney had no doubt he'd betrayed the man, Alexander also knew he hadn't pulled the trigger. Perhaps he'd been indirectly responsible for the man's murder. Yet Patrick had no idea why Joseph had literally fingered him for the crime.

"Listen, Sheriff. Every defendant has a Constitutional right to confront his accuser."

"Sounds to me," Taylor said, "like you did that last night! Let's go, men. Let's get the noble barrister behind bars."

The sheriff, unable to get through the crowd, pulled his gun and pointed it towards the people in his path. At that precise moment, there was absolutely no humor in the peace officer's face. "If you people don't disperse right now," Taylor declared, "then I will drop your dead carcasses right here on this street."

Reluctantly but quickly, the townspeople began to step aside.

"You have to believe me, Sheriff," Alexander pleaded. "I swear I didn't kill Joseph Blakemore."

"As an attorney, Mr. Alexander, you ought to know better than anyone else, that's what the courts are for," Taylor said. "You have my personal guarantee that you'll get fair trial."

"And a real nice hanging," a voice from the crowd shouted.

A few hours later, the headlines of the *Sacramento Union* proclaimed the news that Patrick Alexander had murdered a prominent local businessman.

Chapter Twenty

Wilson Stonegate was indeed a troubled man.

Although he was more than happy to see Patrick Alexander indicted for Blakemore's murder, Stonegate was puzzled as to the reasons why a dying man might have chosen to accuse someone else of *his* crime.

Wilson was certain that Blakemore had no prior knowledge of Alexander's betrayal, not before he showed Joseph the letter that the attorney had passed along to him. There could have been no doubt as to the man's reaction; Blakemore was devastated by the revelation.

Perhaps Joseph mistakenly believed that Malone would eventually identify and track down the president's assassins. Therefore, he ultimately wanted to make sure that the attorney that betrayed him wouldn't go unpunished.

Stonegate certainly saw that idea as plausible.

Still, Wilson didn't believe it. There had to be something more, something that he was just failing to see.

Suddenly, Wilson had another idea.

What if Blakemore had prepared another letter, one that detailed his and Vincent's involvement in the conspiracy on Cleveland's life? If Karen had discovered such a document, she would immediately take it to her husband's trusted attorney, Patrick Alexander.

But doing so would place her life in jeopardy, as well. And Blakemore was definitely smart enough to realize that fact.

Stonegate knew there had to be another letter in Blakemore's office.

Had the sheriff discovered it, Wilson knew that he would've already been arrested. And although Karen had briefly been in the office to identify her husband's writing, he doubted that she had come across the document, either.

That, too, would have resulted in his incarceration.

Stonegate was certain that Blakemore must have left something behind, some kind of document that pointed to his involvement. And he knew it had to be in the man's office.

With all of the people in town for the president's appearance, it was much too risky for someone to be seen going into the room during the day. Moreover, that might also serve to remove some of the suspicion for Blakemore's murder, that Wilson had successfully passed on to the attorney.

Stonegate would order his people to find it tonight.

***

Langston had insisted that the president and his bodyguards were to be given a couple of adjoining rooms in the hotel. But while they were waiting on Kell's return, Clements had insisted that they stick together, manning only one of the rooms.

Once they were inside, Gain quickly moved from window to window, drawing closed the shades, so nobody could be identified from outside the windows of the hotel. It also made it more difficult for a would-be sniper to pick out a target.

After they had been there for a large portion of the day, Langston arranged to have some food and coffee delivered to the room. Their hunger finally satisfied, Gain and Joe patiently waited. The others grew more anxious with every passing hour.

When the knock sounded on their room, Clements drew his six-gun and hid behind the door. Seeing that Carson also had his gun trained on the door, Joe nodded at Langston to open it.

Both men relaxed when Captain Turner entered the room.

He briefly saluted Langston. "Is it okay to speak in front of them, sir?"

"Why not?" Langston replied. "These two men apparently know a lot more about the president's business than I do. I'm just the man's aide."

"As you ordered, sir, I sent some troops to Vincent Fielding's office in San Francisco," Turner said. "The man wasn't there. It looked as if he had been gone for several days. His servants claimed that they know nothing about his current whereabouts."

"Another dead end!" Langston muttered. "Okay, Captain Turner. Instruct your men to keep his place under surveillance. If Fielding returns, detain the man and notify me immediately. Is that clear?"

"Yes, sir," Turner replied.

"What makes you so sure that he's still in San Francisco?" Clements said.

"That's his home."

"Man with his kind of wealth can live anywhere he wants," Joe added. "When he tried to hire me, Fielding was in Denver. Might still be there."

The longer Langston considered Joe's statement, the more sense it made to him. Although Clements was scarcely more than an outlaw, it didn't mean that his idea had no merit. With Cleveland's life on the line, the presidential aide was unwilling to dismiss any suggestion that might lead to ending the conspiracy.

"Captain Turner," Langston said, "it might also be wise to follow Mr. Clements' suggestion. Send some troops to Denver. If Fielding is there, have him arrested. If he has gone, perhaps we can determine his destination."

"I will do it right away, sir," Dent said. "Is there any word on the president?"

"No, there isn't," Langston said. "And frankly, I'm getting a little worried. But you can rest assured, Captain Turner, that you will be among the first to be notified of his arrival."

"Thank you, sir."

While Turner finished talking to Langston, Clements poured himself another cup of coffee, a cup that was much colder now than when it was first delivered. For a moment, he said nothing as he stared at the presidential aide.

He could see the man was worried. In addition, Clements noted that the president's wife was also showing the same signs of insecurity.

"You need to try and relax, Langston," Joe muttered, handing him the cup of coffee he first poured for himself. "President Cleveland's in good hands with Kellen Malone. I would trust the man with my life. Come to think of it, I often have. Even Rachel can confirm that one."

As all eyes turned to her, Rachel nodded.

"Thank you, Joe" Jeremiah said, expressing his gratitude for more than the coffee.

It marked the first time that Langston had addressed Clements by his first name. The fact was not lost on the scar-faced gunman.

"According to Gain, that Callfield kid is a pretty good hand with a gun," Joe added, pouring himself another cup. "Right now, the president is probably a darned sight safer than we are, cooped up like chickens in this hotel room."

"Are you sure he's okay, Mr. Clements?" Frances asked.

"I would bet my life on it, ma'am."

"How did you first come to know him?" the president's wife said.

"When I first met Kellen Malone, I got into a little bit of a shooting scrape with the Palance brothers," Joe explained, tasting his coffee. "It happened in a little saloon down in Austin, Texas."

While they waited on the president's return, Rachel Malone was surprised by the events that were taking place in that room. Clements was a man who rarely talked about himself. As Frances, Gain, and Jeremiah listened to his story, they were learning about an incident that she had never known.

"And Mr. Malone helped you with them," Frances said

"No," Joe replied. "I didn't need his help for that. There were only three of them."

"So what did he do?"

"It turns out that the bartender was some kind of kin to them," he explained. "I never saw him behind me. Malone kept him from cutting me in half with his scatter gun. Next time I saw Malone, he was surrounded by Apaches in the desert. I would've never thought it possible, but the man got us both out of there alive."

"It truly sounds like the two of you are good friends," Frances replied.

"I reckon you could call us that."

***

Grieved by the loss of her husband and mystified by the details of his murder, Karen Blakemore was a woman searching for answers.

For many years, Patrick Alexander had been her husband's attorney, and supposedly, a trusted friend. Why did the man suddenly kill his client?

After her husband's body was found, the sheriff had taken her inside the office to identify the body and to confirm his handwriting. Unfortunately, the circumstances of that most recent visit allowed her no time to search Joseph's office.

She was certain that some cursory search of the contents of Joseph's office had taken place. However, the wife of an attorney, who had been routinely exposed to the law long enough to know that the sheriff was satisfied with simple explanations, knew that the victim's blood-stained identification had been more than sufficient evidence to make an arrest.

If there were any reasonable explanations for these bizarre events, Karen was confident that it would still be found inside.

Hoping nobody would see her enter the room, Karen cautiously looked both ways before entering. The door opened easily under her hand.

Stopping just inside the door, Karen struck a match to light the gas lantern she'd brought along for the task. As the lamp flared, the repulsive scene once again brought tears to her eyes. Karen willed herself to choke them back.

Consciously trying to avoid stepping on her husband's blood stains on the floor, Karen began searching her husband's bookcase, cabinets, and papers. Then she rifled through his appointment books and file folders.

Nothing!

She hesitated at the blood-stained desk.

Finally, the wife of the late Mr. Blakemore realized it couldn't be avoided. She placed the lamp on the edge of the desk. Opening the upper drawers, her search yielded nothing of interest. Karen proceeded to open the lower desk drawer. Longingly, her now-moistened eyes lingered on the whiskey bottle and the glasses beside it.

Overcome by the events of the day, Karen figured the loss of a husband had earned any woman the right to a private drink. The idea brought a brief smile to her face.

Karen lifted the bottle and poured herself a glass. Normally abstaining from the evils of liquor, she downed it in one swallow. As she wiped her eyes and thought about another, her gaze went downward.

Then she saw it.

At the bottom of the drawer, underneath where the liquor bottle had rested, she saw a folded piece of paper. Karen wondered why she hadn't thought of it earlier. Joseph had left his wife one final love note.

The woman quickly unfolded it, expecting to read the words of simple endearment. A sentimental man, Joseph had a way of writing that always touched her heart. His passionate thoughts were evident on every line. She paused long enough to wipe her eyes.

But as she continued to read, Karen was increasingly shocked by the contents. Nothing in life had ever prepared her for the final words of this revelation.

She had read enough for now.

Although she hadn't yet reached the end, Karen had seen enough to make it plain that her husband had been engaged in a dreadful conspiracy on President Cleveland's life. Moreover, there could be no doubt that his involvement in the conspiracy ultimately led to his murder.

From reading the note, it was apparent that a remorseful Joseph had wanted out. Perhaps he had been killed because the others feared that he would expose them. Apparently, his attorney had also shared some involvement.

As much as she wanted to read the entire letter, Karen was smart enough to realize that this knowledge also placed her life in jeopardy. If the letter was found to be in her possession, the men who tried to kill Cleveland would also try to kill her.

There would be time to finish it later.

Frantically folding the note and stuffing it in the folds of her skirt, Karen doused the light, feeling her way towards the door.

At that moment, she heard a noise outside the office.

Moving to a place behind the door, Karen lurked in the darkness. The door began to open. The woman's heart beat so swiftly, she feared that the person entering the darkened room would hear its pounding.

Instantly, she hoped the intruder would enter the room, leaving the door open behind him. Then, she could just quietly slip outside, unnoticed in the darkness.

Her plan was thwarted nearly as soon as she conceived it.

Using his foot to kick the door closed behind him, the intruder began to noisily fumble around in the darkness for a lamp. Certain that her life would end in the same place her husband drew his last tortured breath, a terrified Mrs. Blakemore clung to the wall like a portrait.

Unlike the intruder, whose eyes had yet to become adjusted to the darkness, Karen squinted to pick up his movements.

The intruder was about to turn on the lamp.

Realizing that discovery meant certain death, she dreaded the idea of their orphaned children. Losing two parents in less than twenty-four hours, the thought only served to spur her anger. The woman in Karen feared; the mother acted.

Remembering the lamp she was holding, Karen slowly and silently inched forward. Once she was in reach, the woman swung the lamp, with all of the force she could muster, across the back of the man's head.

The intruder went down in a heap, groaning from the pain.

Karen stumbled over the man's fallen body as she searched for the door handle. Throwing the door open, the woman saw her escape. But the moment she started through the door to safety, a strong hand caught hold of her ankle.

She kicked at the man and tried to pull away, but he clung to the woman's leg like iron shackles. Despite the painful explosions taking place in his battered skull, the man's strength prevailed, pulling the woman to the floor.

Karen shrieked and cried, but there was nobody around to hear them. The man, still fighting unconsciousness, tried to pull himself on top of her. The intruder smelled of stale sweat and liquor. The woman tried to push him away as he reached for his gun.

She kicked at him; she battered the man with her fists. In the midst of the struggle, the gun clattered away from his hand into the darkness. Her teeth made the intruder scream like a wounded animal. Yet his grip on the woman tightened.

Confident that she was going to die, she struggled to get away from the man. Despite his wounds, the man's strength was still too much for her. His fingers, moistened by blood and sweat, began to tighten around her neck. Her clothes became torn in the brutal scuffle. The woman clamored for her next breath.

In her mind, Karen saw the faces of her children.

Once more, the memory of her children inspired her fierce desire to live. Summoning her last ounce of strength, she fought to get her arms free. She found his cruel face in the darkness and tried to claw the man's eyes from their sockets. Crying out in pain, the man clutched at his wounded and bleeding eyeballs.

At the release of his grip, Karen finally broke free. Picking up an object that had fallen to the floor during their struggle, the woman brutally smashed the item against his head. Under her breath, the woman prayed that she killed him. The intruder made no further moves to stop her.

Stopping only long enough to confirm that the letter was still in her possession, Karen ran out into the night. She paused to hide in the shadows, listening to see if anyone was trailing along behind her.

Hearing nothing, Karen knew what she must do. Vincent Fielding and Wilson Stonegate must pay for their crimes and for the murder of her husband. But their men would be coming to find her. First, she knew she must reach her children and get them to safety.

As she disappeared into the darkness, Karen softly cursed the name of Joseph Blakemore, the strong and tarnished man that she still loved.

Chapter Twenty-One

As nightfall came, Langston and the president's wife became increasingly more concerned about her husband's safety. All of them knew that Cameron Ellis was still on the loose. And the man had already made two attempts on Cleveland's life. In addition, they were all aware that Kell had previously stated his firm belief that Ellis would eventually try again.

What nobody other than Clements knew, Malone had actually stated that Ellis would never rest until he killed President Cleveland or died in the attempt.

Leaving Carson with the president's people, Joe had ventured out into the city. Because it was commonly known that Clements often walked on the wrong side of the law, he was able to glean information from those who wouldn't speak to ordinary lawmen.

"Do you suppose Mr. Clements is okay?" Frances said. "He's been gone a couple hours."

"Trust me," Rachel said. "Although their actions often frighten me, Joe Clements and my husband were made for moments such as these.

"Kell is a kind and gentle man, who would prefer to live peaceably with everyone. Joe Clements is a hard and lonely soul, who trusts almost no one," she explained. "One abides by the law; the other has been known to hold nothing but contempt for lawmen. But despite their differences, those two men are strikingly similar."

As Rachel moved deeper into her story, Jeremiah moved his chair closer to the conversation. While still keeping his eye trained on the door, Carson divided his attention, tuning a listening ear to the information about an old and trusted friend.

"How could two men such as that become friends?" Frances asked. "They seem so different."

"Not in the ways that truly matter."

"What do you mean, Rachel?"

"You remember the story that Joe told you earlier, about him meeting Kell in the desert?" Rachel continued, pausing to taste her coffee. "There was something in that story that Joe *didn't* tell you. He probably held back that information on purpose. Not long after those two happened upon each other, Joe was hired to kill my husband."

"Since your husband is helping us, Mr. Clements obviously didn't take the job," Frances said, with a smile.

"Not because he didn't think he was capable," Rachel replied. "Joe Clements is a proud man. So is my husband. But it was their time together in the wilderness, their days spent battling hostile Apaches, fighting alongside one another, and trying to survive, the conditions created a special kind of kinship between the two of them. I can't even pretend to understand it; but I recognize that it truly exists."

"That often happens in war times," Gain declared, softly. "When men bear arms against a common enemy, there comes a time when they no longer fight for the flag and their homeland. They fight for each other. It sometimes forms a bond stronger than blood."

"You sound like you're speaking from experience, Mr. Carson," Jeremiah said.

"More than I care to admit, Mr. Langston," he said. "And please excuse me for interrupting you, Miss Rachel."

"Think nothing of it, Gain. A man's perspective added some clarity to what I was trying to explain to Frances," she said. "My father was a hard, but gentle man. He served in the war. He knew the hardship and atrocities of the battlefield. But it was my relationship with him that helped me to understand my husband, and those like him.

"Kell and Joe are kind but dangerous men. But they are men of honor, to a code known only to themselves, or to a loyalty borne to each other," she added, with a gentle smile. "Trust me, Frances. Your fears should be reserved for those who would seek to harm them."

Suddenly, a knock sounded on the door.

Upon hearing the sound, Gain grabbed iron as he moved to the side of the door. Langston armed himself with a double barrel shotgun.

Jeremiah brought the weapon to his shoulder. He nodded at Carson. Gently moving the chair that was propped up under the knob, Gain eased open the door.

"Are you going to open the door, you old horse rustler," Joe said, "or just leave me sleeping out in this hallway all night?"

"Come on in, Joe."

Jeremiah and Gain lowered their weapons, as a smiling Joe Clements stood in the doorway.

"And look what I found, skulking around in the darkness."

Joe stepped inside the door and was followed by President Cleveland and Kellen Malone. Joining them were Slate Callfield, Jesse Malone, and Buck Halstead. Denton Turner was only a couple of moments behind.

The next few minutes resembled a family reunion.

"It's good to see you, my dear," Cleveland said, firmly embracing his wife. "The last few hours were truly the greatest adventure of my life!"

Rachel rushed over to hug her husband, their lips melting together. Then the woman quickly moved to embrace Jesse and Buck, as well.

Handshakes and introductions soon followed.

"I hope we don't have to pay all of them, too," Langston muttered, softly.

"Jeremiah," Cleveland said, "these men have proven to be worth everything we give them. I can only hope that future presidents are shielded by men such as these."

After Langston made sure that a couple of pots of fresh coffee were delivered to their room, Kell and the president related the details of their trip.

Joe listened silently, chewing on a cold biscuit. "It's lucky you didn't get off the train this morning, Mr. President. After talking to some of the people in town, I learned that there were about three gunmen, waiting for you at the depot." He cast a brief glance towards Langston. "If Malone hadn't taken him off the train, the president would be a dead man right now."

"I've learned my lesson," Jeremiah said, startled by this latest revelation. "I won't question Kell's decisions again. I won't question yours either, Joe."

The slight trace of a smile appeared on Clements' lips.

"Were you able to find out who hired them?" Kell said.

"Couldn't learn a thing about that," Joe replied. "Looks like we're still in the dark."

"The president will never be safe," Gain said, "until we kill or capture everybody involved in this thing."

"And right now," Langston added, "we don't know a lot more than when we started."

"What's worse," Slate said, "we still don't know the location of Cameron Ellis. He's the one I want!"

"Heard one other thing in town tonight," Joe said. "There was some businessman killed in his office last night. Don't think it has anything to do with us, though. The man was murdered by his own lawyer, like I needed any more reason to hate that profession. The dead man's name was Blakemore."

"Joseph Blakemore?" Langston blustered.

"Yes," Joe said. "That was the name. It mean something to you?"

"I know what you're thinking, Jeremiah," President Cleveland said, quickly thumbing through the document that Langston had given him. "There it is. Joseph Blakemore. His name's on the list of those who obtained fraudulently acquired public lands. Vincent Fielding is also on that list."

"That can't be a coincidence!" Langston declared. "His murder has to be connected to the threats on the president's life."

"I'm with you on this one, Langston," Kell stated. "Who did you say killed Blakemore."

"The guy's name is Patrick Alexander. They've already held a trial for the man. The lawyer swears he didn't do it, but he won't say who did," Joe stated. "Folks on the jury didn't believe him. The evidence must have been pretty good, too. Only took them about ten minutes to convict Alexander."

"Maybe we ought to go talk to him in the morning," Kell said.

"Couldn't hurt," Joe added. "And right now, it's the only thing we've got. Don't think we want to wait too long, though."

"Why's that?"

"Evidently, the dead man had a lot of friends in town," Joe explained. "Some of them wanted to skip the trial and move right to the execution. And they already have that gallows built, down by the train yard."

"It's been a long day, Joe," Kell said. "I'm sure it'll wait until morning. We'll take turns standing guard. You and Gain care to take the first watch?"

"Fine with me," Joe replied. "Get some shuteye."

Gain took a seat over next to the door. "My old pappy used to tell me that things always look better in the morning."

"Hope your old man was right," Kell said.

"Not usually," Gain added.

Chapter Twenty-Two

Vincent Fielding was still furious about the events of the other night. Twice he had been humiliated by a young man with scarcely the mind of a child. Fielding's vanity demanded that he have the boy killed; his common sense told him that now was not the time.

Billy would have to wait. So would Jenny.

Vincent had already learned that there were troops searching for him at his San Francisco home and office. His wife and children knew nothing about his activities. Then the word came to him that there were soldiers headed for his Denver location, as well.

Fielding wasn't worried.

He was certain that nobody knew about the spacious mountain cabin, that he'd built to his specifications several years ago. And in preparation for just this set of circumstances, Vincent had funds deposited in several Western banks. That made them easy to access, if he was ever pursued by the authorities.

Fielding had grown accustomed to a certain style of living, that only required his wife and kids as stage props in a drama. He had no plans to let President Cleveland or anybody else take his lifestyle or manner of living away.

"We've got the wagon packed to leave," Kansas Jack said, still carrying the bruises that Billy's hands administered to him the other night. "Is there anything else you want me to do?"

"Yes, Jack," Fielding groused. "Do your best to stay away from the dummy. He's liable to kill you the next time you show your face at the saloon."

Kansas Jack merely scowled and returned to his duties.

Another one of Fielding's employees, Tally Jenkins, a short man with a tied-down gun, came into the room. He was carrying a piece of paper.

"Mr. Fielding," Tally said, "this note just came in from the telegraph office."

Fielding began to smile as he read the few words on the note:

I'll take him tomorrow. C.E.

Ever since his failed attempt to kill the president in Cheyenne, Fielding had been unaware of Cameron Ellis' location. He was pleased to learn the man was still alive. Better still, he was delighted to learn that Ellis had arrived in Sacramento.

He knew the man well enough to know that, once he'd be paid for a job, nothing would keep Cam Ellis from completing the mission.

Fielding had only to leave for now. If the troops were unable to find him, they would return to their base in a matter of days. Then he would restore his base of operations to Denver. And if the president were to be killed, then the troops might pull out much earlier.

It would probably leave the entire military in disarray.

Since Thomas Hendricks, Cleveland's vice president, had succumbed to poor health after only eight months, the office had remained vacant. Although the Constitution provided for a line of succession, Fielding knew an assassination might throw the government into turmoil for several months following the president's death.

He figured that an enterprising young businessman could easily exploit the situation for personal gain.

At this point, Fielding no longer cared if Cleveland actually returned those railroad lands to the public. The fact that he was simply pursuing the notion was reason enough to want the man dead. Tomorrow, the man would pay the ultimate price for his arrogance.

And after Ellis completed the contract on Cleveland's life, Vincent determined that Kellen Malone, the man who interfered with his plans, should be the next to die.

Fielding smiled at the thought. Then his mind returned to Jenny, the desirable woman that had fallen in love with the killer, Skull Clements.

***

Leaving Gain and Callfield to look after the president, Kell and Joe went to the jail to talk to the condemned attorney. After requiring them to check their guns at the desk, the sheriff took them back to Alexander's cell. Then he left them alone.

"I'm Kellen Malone," he said, "and this is…"

Patrick cut him off before he could finish his sentence. "I know who you are, Mr. Malone. And the man with you, with the scar on his face, he must be the notorious Skull Clements. Everybody in town has heard of you. Now, what do you want?"

"We have reason to believe," Kell said, "that you might have some knowledge of the attempts on the president's life."

"I have no idea where you acquired that information, but you are clearly mistaken."

"I think you're a liar," Joe said.

"Here lately, I have been accused of worse things," he muttered.

"Joseph Blakemore was recently named to a list of men who gained control of government lands by illegal means," Kell explained. "After the president announced his intention to return those lands to the public, the attempts on his life began. Then, you killed Blakemore. You can see why we might think there's a connection."

"That's certainly an intriguing story you tell, Mr. Malone. But I would have no difficulty ripping it apart in the courtroom," Alexander said, sitting on his bunk, as he leaned back against the wall. "But in case you haven't heard, I didn't kill Joseph Blakemore."

"That isn't what the jury thought," Joe replied.

"As someone who has been an attorney for nearly all of my adult life," Mr. Clements, "I can tell you that juries occasionally get things wrong."

"Well, you seem pretty calm for an innocent man facing a hangman's rope," Kell said.

"You're not listening to me, Mr. Malone. I didn't say I was innocent," he muttered. "But I did say that I didn't kill Joseph Blakemore. There is a difference."

Joe had heard enough. "Let's get out of here, Malone! This is a waste of time."

Malone's patience was running thin, too. "What are you talking about, Alexander?"

"An innocent man does not betray his client," he explained. "Somebody else killed the man. Yet it was my betrayal of Joseph that ultimately led to his death. That betrayal will lead to my execution, as well. Apparently, it was fate."

"Well, if you didn't pull the trigger, why did Blakemore take the time to accuse you of his murder?"

"As a former resident of Yuma Prison, Mr. Malone, you would know that sitting in a jail cell gives a man a lot of time to think," Alexander said. "And I have been doing a lot of that lately. As you have already concluded, Joseph knew things about the conspiracy on the president's life. Foolishly, he chose to write them down and give them to me. And I gave that note to his killer.

"But suppose for a minute that the copy he gave me wasn't the only one he left," the lawyer continued. "What if his wife were to find it? Maybe Joseph knew that she would bring it to his lawyer, the one man

188

that her husband trusted. Then, to protect my interests, I would have found it necessary to have her killed, too.

"Joseph Blakemore was a man with no shortage of faults. But there could be no question that he loved his wife, Karen. Blakemore's final words, written in his own blood, were designed to protect her from meeting the same fate as he experienced."

"Well, who pulled the trigger?" Kell said.

"That I can't tell you."

"Can't, or won't?" Joe asked.

"That is a distinction without a difference," Patrick said. "If I tell you, then the man will have me killed, too."

"But you're going to die, anyway," Kell replied.

"You may not believe this, Mr. Malone, but I used to be an honorable man," he said. "I have already betrayed one trust; I will not betray another. Unlike the two of you, I am by no means a brave man. But if restoring my honor means that I have to take that knowledge to the grave, then I will do it. That is definitely the fate I deserve."

"Good luck with that!" Joe declared, shaking his head. "Ain't nothing noble about dancing at the end of a noose."

Patrick Alexander stood to his feet and walked over to the cell door. He placed both hands on the bars, looking Kell directly in the eye.

"I truly hope you succeed in your efforts to bring the conspirators to justice, Mr. Malone. I just won't do anything to help you." Alexander pushed away from the bars, cupping his hand alongside his mouth. "Sheriff! Sheriff!" he shouted. "Get these men out of here now."

"We'll be seeing you, Mr. Alexander," Kell said.

"Not for long," the lawyer replied.

Kell and Joe started past the other cells, the sheriff meeting them halfway. "Hope you boys were able to get what you need," he said.

"Not really," Kell said, as the two of them slung their gunbelts around their hips.

"If I can do anything to help you," the sheriff said, "let me know."

"Thanks, Sheriff," Kell said, shaking the man's hand.

Clements also returned the lawman's handshake.

When Kell and Joe left the sheriff's office, they paused outside the door. Neither of them spoke for a moment, enjoying the stillness of a new morning. Joe began to roll a smoke, lighting it with a match struck on the porch railing.

"You know the man was telling the truth, don't you?"

"Don't much matter to me," Joe stated, grimly. "A man who betrays his friends deserves to hang."

At that moment, a man holding a pencil and paper came running down the sidewalk towards them.

"My name is Kayden Winchester," he said. "I am a reporter for the *Sacramento Union*."

"I'm sorry to hear that for you," Joe replied, blowing a thin trail of smoke in the reporter's round face.

Undeterred, the reporter excitedly said, "You must be Skull Clements, the gunman!"

"Some people call me that," Joe said, with a look of contempt "The dead ones."

"And you must be Kellen Malone," Kayden blustered. "What is it like to kill that that many men?"

"You're about to find out," Kell stated, looking at the man with the same regard he would give an annoying house fly.

As the two men tried to walk away from him, he quickly moved to block their path. The reporter continued, oblivious to the danger of receiving a severe beating at their hands.

"The whole town is buzzing about your arrival," he said. "Kellen Malone, Skull Clements, Gain Carson, and Marshal Slate Callfield—all of them are in one place, at one time, protecting the President of the United States. This is the most famous gathering of guns since Wyatt Earp, Charlie Bassett, Bat Masterson, and Bill Tilghman rode on the same posse."

Kell said nothing as he pushed past the man. Joe paused, only long enough to put the flaming end of his cigarette into the reporter's coat pocket. Then, he resumed walking.

As gunfire rang out down the street, the two men broke into a run.

Chapter Twenty-Three

Like carrion over a corpse, Cameron Ellis had been watching the hotel since several hours before daylight.

Kellen Malone and Joe Clements had already left the hotel some time earlier. The big guy, who Ellis learned was named Halstead, had left to catch the morning stage. Licking his lips at the opportunity it offered, Cam smiled when he saw Gain Carson go downstairs for coffee.

If things went the way he hoped, Cam thought he might bag more game that just the president. Maybe he'd also have the chance to kill Malone's wife and son.

Ellis silently made his way up the back steps. Seeing Denton Turner in the hallway, he slipped up behind the soldier. A strong hand clamped over the captain's mouth, as the other hand plunged the knife deep into his lower back. Cam buried the blade to its hilt.

Turner was helpless.

Lowering the man's nearly-lifeless body to the floor, Cam wiped the bloody knife on the man's uniform. Then, he knocked lightly.

Knowing that Turner was stationed at the door, and thinking that Gain had returned with the coffee, Slate opened the door without thinking.

Cam thrust the knife into the young lawman, drawing blood.

With the blade still inside his body, Slate caught the assassin by the arms. Wincing at the pain, Slate wrestled the man out into the hallway.

"We need to go out the window," Jesse said.

Upon hearing the boy's suggestion, Langston sprang into action. He caught up the shotgun and slammed the door closed behind them. Then he and Jesse shoved a dresser in front of the door as a barricade.

Urging the president out the window onto the rooftop, Cleveland insisted that the women and Jesse go first. Figuring there was no point in arguing with the man, Langston helped Frances, Rachel, and Jesse through the window. Satisfied, Cleveland followed them outside. Then Langston scrambled out the window with the shotgun.

Frightened customers threw open their doors at the disturbance. They quickly ducked back inside the safety of their rooms, when they saw the dead body and the two men grappling like bulls in a pasture.

Ellis tried to pull his gun, but Slate's arms held the man like a steel trap. He slammed the gunman backward, loosing the plaster from the walls.

Despite his injuries, the younger marshal's strength was too much for the man. He flung the gunman around the hallway like a child's ragdoll. As the gunman tripped over Turner's body, Slate came down on top of him. Thinking only of his friend, Aiden Frye, Callfield wrenched the knife from his own body and plunged it deep into the outlaw.

Ellis ceased his struggle. Then he was still.

Exhausted from the battle and from his loss of blood, Callfield tried to rise to his feet. Then, he collapsed on the floor beside the fallen gunman.

As the young marshal lie unconscious in the hallway, Ellis suddenly regained his senses. He struggled to stand. Once more, he tried the door. Realizing the door had been barricaded, Ellis lowered his shoulder and finally forced his way into the room.

With the windows open and the curtains draped outside the window, Ellis knew President Cleveland had fled his quarters.

Drawing his gun, Ellis stuck his head out the window.

He quickly ducked back inside the room, narrowly missing the single blast from Langston's shotgun. The shards of glass stung his face and momentarily blinded him. Frantically, Cam rubbed his eyes. He was fully aware that Langston still had another barrel.

Out on the second floor rooftop, Jesse was searching for a way down. A terrified Langston boldly shielded the president and the women from danger. Unflinchingly, his shotgun was shouldered and trained on the window. The man's shirt soaked with sweat, Langston waited for the gunman to once again show his face.

Jeremiah prayed that his aim would be better next time. He prayed that help would arrive. He prayed that he would live, that they would all live.

On the second floor of the building, a couple of the hotel's other customers hurried to the downed marshal's aid. One of them scrambled downstairs to find the sheriff. As the remaining helpers knelt beside the young man, Slate heard the shotgun blast

"Help me up! Help me up now!" he demanded. "Then get out of here."

Unwilling to argue with the injured marshal, they helped the fallen man to his feet. Then they heeded Callfield's orders, running for the safety of the stairs.

Slate grabbed iron and ran into the president's room.

Sensing the threat from behind, Ellis wheeled around and began firing. His gun stabbed flame at the marshal. With his eyesight still unclear from the shattered window glass, Cam's first shots failed to find his target. The bullet tore through the wall, injuring a fleeing resident.

Unlike the assassin, Slate's aim was true. His gun rang out, again and again. The slugs staggered the outlaw. They tore at Cam's chest and lungs. One pierced his neck.

Still, the gunman remained on his feet.

Outside the window, Langston heard the shooting taking place inside. He swallowed hard, hoping that a couple of his prayers had been answered.

Fearful the Lord might be toying with him, Langston kept the gun shouldered. His eye never left the window.

Remaining upright due to the power of sheer evil, Cam's gun returned fire. His slug creased Slates's side. Another blast caught the young marshal in the fleshy part of his leg.

As Slate continued to fire, the young marshal sensed another man there beside him. That man was firing too.

Joining Callfield in the battle, Kellen Malone began to blaze away at Cam Ellis, riddling his body with bullets. Malone's twin sixes flamed, over and over. The gunman's body trembled with every repeated impact.

The fierce barrage of gunfire drove Cam's motionless body backward. As he slipped to the floor, he left an ugly crimson stain down the face of the wall. The gun clang to his hand

Although his gun was empty, Slate continued to advance on the gunman. He triggered his six-gun, the hammer striking on spent chambers. With his heavy loss of blood, the young marshal swayed from side to side, as he towered over the dead body of Cameron Ellis.

By this time, Gain had entered the room. "It's okay, kid," he said, gently removing the empty revolver from Slate's hand. His brow furrowed at the sight of the weakened young man. "You got him, Slate. Now, let's get you some help."

Joe Clements rushed to his other side, assisting Gain in getting the young man down the stairs, and over to the doctor's office.

With the toe of his boot, Kell kicked the gun away from Cam's outstretched hand. He squatted on his haunches to confirm the man was dead. His thoughts immediately returned to his wife and son.

"Rachel! Rachel!" Kell shouted. "Jesse!"

"I'm fine, Kell" Rachel replied, walking over to the window. "We all are, thanks to Langston and Jesse."

"And Slate Callfield," he added.

Malone took Rachel's hand and helped her back in the window. Conscious of how close he might have come to losing the woman he loved, Kell threw his arms around her. Then he offered his assistance to the others, stopping just long enough to hug his son. Langston was the last to reenter the window.

Kell thrust out his hand. "Thank you, Jeremiah. I owe you."

Langston merely laughed. "It was your son's idea."

"That's quite a family you have, Mr. Malone," the president stated. "Your wife and son displayed remarkable courage. And, Jeremiah, I don't know how I can ever thank you for all you did for Frances and me."

"You're welcome, sir," Langston said, looking around the room. "What happened in here?"

"Ellis stabbed Dent and Callfield. Dent's dead," Kell explained, his eyes showing the remorse over the loss of a trusted friend. "Somehow, the kid got to his feet. I still don't know how he managed to do it. The gun battle had already started when I came into the room. I got off a couple of shots before Ellis went down."

"Can't say I'm sorry to see the man dead," Langston observed.

"Where's Mr. Callfield?" Cleveland said.

"Joe and Gain took him over to the doctor's office," Kell added, thumbing fresh shells into his gun. Rachel sat beside him on the bed, her hand touching his arm. "I have no idea if the kid will even make it. But from what I saw in this room a couple of minutes ago, I wouldn't bet against him pulling through."

When the hotel manager barged into the room, he was immediately covered by the guns of Kell and Langston. Startled by the sight, the man thrust his arms into the air, to show that he meant them no harm. Their guns lowered. His breathing returned to normal. Surveying the carnage inside the room, the manager's face turned a sickly green.

"Mr. President, if you and your guests would care to follow me," he said, "I can offer you a couple of nice rooms down the hall. Please accept my apologies, sir. This shouldn't have happened in our fair city."

"Unfortunately," the president said, "we are starting to grow accustomed to it."

Outside the door, about a dozen blue-clad troops lined the hallways. A couple of the soldiers were removing the dead body of Captain Turner. As Kell removed his hat for the fallen soldier and friend, the president saluted. Rachel wept.

Nobody dared to break the silence of the moment.

After pausing to honor the fallen, the manager continued down the hallway. He was soon joined by the others. He pointed to a couple of rooms. "These are yours, Mr. President. I hope the rest of your stay will be uneventful."

"So do I," Cleveland said.

About that time, Clements returned from taking Slate to the doctor's office. His shirt was stained with the blood of the young marshal.

"How's he doing?" Kell said.

"The doctor isn't sure," Joe stated. "Gain is still with him."

"Several good men have died," Kell said, "because I didn't kill Ellis when I first had the chance. "Let's hope Gain's son-in-law isn't one of them."

Just then, the president had a thought. "Mr. Clements, there's a physician in town named William Leftridge," Cleveland said. "He's undoubtedly the finest surgeon in the state. If you would be so kind, I want you to locate the man, and take him to see Callfield. Tell Dr. Leftridge to send me the bill. If he refuses to come, feel free to tell Mr. Carson. I have a hunch that Gain might be very persuasive in this case."

"He just might, at that," Clements said, with a laugh. Joe grabbed his hat and started for the door. "I'll be back in a little while."

Just then, one of soldiers knocked on the door. "I'm sorry to bother you, sir," he said. "There's a woman out here who wants to talk to Mr. Malone. I tried to get her to come back, but she was insistent."

Cleveland looked over at Malone for confirmation.

Kell nodded.

"Send her in," the president said.

Entering the room was an attractive woman, holding a bloody, folded piece of paper. Her obviously expensive garments were soiled, torn, and spotted with blood. Rachel quickly removed her shawl and rushed to place it around the visitor.

"Thank you so much," the woman said. "I apologize for my appearance." She looked at Jesse and the three gentlemen in the room. "Which one of you is Kellen Malone?"

"I am Malone," Kell said.

"Pleased to meet you," the woman said. "My name is Karen Blakemore."

Chapter Twenty-Four

"It is my understanding," Karen said, "that you, Mr. Malone, are the one responsible for protecting the president."

"Yes, I am. Call me Kell," Malone replied. "And please take your time. If you'll pardon me for saying so, ma'am, you look nearly done in."

"I had a rough night."

"Lot of that going around," Malone added.

"I am President Cleveland," he said, gently offering his hand to the woman. "We heard about your husband, ma'am. Please allow me to express my sorrow for your loss."

"Thank you, Mr. President. But you may not feel so charitable," she replied, "as soon as you learn my reason for being here."

The woman sat down on the bed, as the others gathered around to hear her story.

"I was almost killed in trying to recover this," Karen said, handing the letter over to Malone. "Then I had to spend the night hiding my children."

Kell said nothing as he read the note.

"Unknown to me," Karen said, looking at the president, "my late husband was involved in the conspiracy to kill you, sir."

"It's all there, Mr. President," Kell stated. "Vincent Fielding was behind the attempts on your life. So was the woman's husband, Mr. Blakemore. Helping them was a man named Wilson Stonegate."

"Wilson Stonegate," Langston said, "was another name on the list, Mr. President."

Cleveland nodded.

Malone passed it to Langston, who later handed it to the president. Cleveland read the note, folded it, and returned it to the woman.

"I think it was someone, working for Stonegate, who almost killed me last night."

"What happened?"

"I was in my husband's office late last evening when I found the letter. Just as I was about to leave, someone came in the room," she said. "I tried to hide in the darkness. But there was no chance to get away. Then we struggled in the darkness for a time. I still don't know how I got away from him. I clawed at his eyes and struck him with something."

"You're lucky to be alive, ma'am," Kell said. "But what made you decide to bring the note to me?"

"I just didn't know who could be trusted in this town," Karen explained. "Fielding and Stonegate are powerful men. Apparently, they had Patrick kill my husband."

"With all due respect ma'am," Kell declared, "I don't think the lawyer killed your husband. Alexander swears he didn't do it. And after seeing this note, I'm absolutely sure of it."

"How can that be?" Karen asked. "Joseph wrote the man's name in his own blood."

"I know he did, ma'am. But I believe he did that to protect you."

"That can't be right. A jury found him guilty."

"Let me try this another way," Kell said. "Suppose for a second that Joseph died before he could write anything on the desk? And then later, you found the note. Under those circumstances, what would you have done with it?"

"I suppose I would have taken it to Patrick."

"That's exactly what I am saying. Your husband knew that you trusted Alexander; he trusted him, too. And it was that trust that got him killed," he said. "Somewhere along the way, I think your husband had a change of heart. He wanted to expose the conspiracy.

"Unfortunately, he chose to share those plans with his attorney," Kell continued. "Then I think Alexander told Stonegate what Joseph was planning. Not long after that, Stonegate killed him. If that wasn't bad enough, Stonegate even testified against the man, claiming he saw the lawyer coming out of his office."

"Yes," Langston offered, "I'm sure Wilson was more than happy to let the lawyer take the blame for his crime. After all, who would believe the attorney? The court's best witness was the victim's own testimony."

"So you're saying that Joseph knew I would find the note?" Karen said, the full meaning of her husband's deed settling on her mind. "And he feared that I would take it to Patrick, which would have led to me being killed, too."

"Yes, ma'am," Kell stated. "That's what I think happened."

"Joseph's final deed was an act of love and protection," Rachel added. "He must have loved you very much."

"If what you say is correct," she stated, "then Patrick will be hanged for a crime he didn't commit. Shouldn't we try and do something?"

"I believe Mr. Malone's theory is certainly credible," Cleveland said. "But all we have right now is supposition. I doubt that it would be enough to reverse the ruling."

"And Patrick's conviction would provide enough reasonable doubt," Langston explained, "that any jury would easily acquit Mr. Stonegate for the murder of your husband."

"Alexander made his bed," Kell replied, harshly. "Now it's time for him to sleep in it!"

"But if you're correct," Karen muttered, "then Stonegate will go unpunished for Joseph's murder."

"You can rest assured that isn't going to happen, ma'am!" Kell declared, checking his twin six-guns. "As soon as I'm done talking to you, I'm personally going after Wilson Stonegate. He can surrender or die where he stands. At this moment, it doesn't really make much difference to me. And I doubt that he has any real desire to meet up with Gain Carson right now.

"Now that Stonegate's involvement has been fully exposed, he shouldn't have any further reason to try and kill you, Mrs. Blakemore. But I'd feel better if you stayed here for now," Kell continued. "After he's been brought to justice, then you can safely return to your home and family. Vincent Fielding's already left California. So, he shouldn't be any threat to you. But his day's coming soon."

Malone returned the hat to his head. Before starting for the door, he leaned over and softly kissed his wife.

"You be careful, Kell," Rachel said.

"I will," he said. "Jesse, you and Langston look after things here. Be back soon."

"God be with you," Cleveland said.

"He sure isn't with them," Kell replied

***

Upon learning that an unknown woman had been in Blakemore's office, Wilson Stonegate was certain that the person who escaped that room had been Karen Blakemore. In addition, he was also confident that there must have been another letter, something in the room that pointed to his guilt, in the conspiracy to assassinate President Cleveland.

Stonegate's men spent all night trying to locate Blakemore's wife. They even tried to find her children, hoping to flush the woman out of hiding.

All of it was to no avail.

Like Vincent Fielding, Stonegate had no other option than to flee Sacramento.

It was only a matter of time before the authorities came for him. Furiously, Wilson was shoving clothes into an expensive carpet bag. Stonegate also removed a gun from the dresser and stuck it inside the bag. Another gun was tucked into the waist of his pants, hidden by his coat.

As Malone approached Stonegate's place, just outside of town, a pair of Wilson's men met him just inside the gate. One of them was holding a rifle in the crook of his arm. The other man was wearing a fresh bandage on his head and another on his left eye.

"Who are you?" the man with the rifle said. "And what do you want?"

"I'm Kellen Malone. I'm here to see Wilson Stonegate."

"Kellen Malone, huh? What if Stonegate doesn't want to see you?"

"He's going to see me, one way or the other," Malone declared. "I would prefer to do it the easy way. But hard works for me, too."

"What if we try to stop you?"

"Then you'll die."

The man with the rifle elbowed the other man. "One man alone, against two guns. You've got grit, Malone; I'll give you that. But what happens if we just kill you?"

"You so much as even lift that rifle, I'll kill you."

The man with the rifle stared Malone in the eye. Like many of those in the West, he was familiar with the man's reputation. Stonegate's guard saw that his arms hung loosely at his side, next to the twin holsters. He saw no fear in the man. He saw no humor. There was only resolve.

Although Malone's attention was directed at the man with the rifle, his eyes also covered the man with the bandages. Something in his manner led Kell to believe that he might be the more dangerous of the two.

"Are you two men going to step aside and let me pass, or do I have to kill you?"

Just then, the man with the bandages went for his gun. His draw was swift and clean, but only a second too slow. Matching the speed from a rattlesnake's strike, Malone's guns were already up and firing, placing two slugs in the man's chest.

The man with the bandages hit the ground dead.

Upon hearing the sound of gunfire, Stonegate decided that he had packed enough belongings. Everything else could wait. Frantically, Wilson closed his bag and headed for the back door of the house.

The man holding the rifle never saw Kell draw. He never even had a chance to move. Then he saw the muzzles of Kell's twin six-guns pointed directly at his chest. Just as quickly, Malone holstered the guns.

"You care to try?" Malone said.

Beads of sweat were breaking out on the man's head. As he tried to swallow, his throat felt as dry as powder. The rifle seemed to be growing heavy in his arms.

"What will people say about me if I don't try?"

"Who cares what they say?"

"I do," the man declared. "I still have my pride."

"But you won't have tomorrow."

"What do you mean by that?"

"If you walk away, you can worry about what they might say about you tomorrow," Kell explained, softly. "There are no more tomorrows for your friend, here. It's not too late for you. Tell me something, kid. What will your pride be worth to you when you're pushing up sod?"

Stonegate's guard took another downward glance at the lifeless body of his friend, next to his feet. He suddenly longed for a cool drink of water.

"What you say, mister, it kind of makes sense to me."

"That's good, kid. I really don't want to kill you."

"You know I'm not afraid of you, don't you, Malone?"

"I know that. You look like a brave young man. Probably a smart one, too," he added. "If I could give you some advice, it would be to stay clear of the Arizona territory. I don't ever want to see you again."

Fearful of even moving his hands to point, the young man motioned with his head. "My horse is over there by the rail, Malone. You promise you won't shoot me, if I ride out of here."

"You have my word," Kell said. "I'm only here for Stonegate."

"Then you will find him inside,' the frightened young man said. "You don't mind if I take my rifle, do you?"

"Every man needs a long gun."

The young man started to leave, but stopped. "What about my friend, there? Would you see that he gets a proper burial?"

"You have my word on that, too."

"Thanks, mister. Thanks for everything," he said, walking towards his horse.

The young man untied the horse, swung himself into the saddle, and reined the horse in a northern direction. Casting a backward glance at Malone, he suddenly placed the horse in a run. He didn't slow down until the man was merely a small speck in his past.

Then the young man thought about the future. Tomorrow! The word brought a smile to his face.

Kellen Malone smiled as he watched the young man ride away towards the far horizon. There had been enough killing for today. He hoped to be through with it. But that decision wasn't up to him; it was up to Wilson Stonegate.

As he approached the front of the house, he saw that the door was locked. Drawing his guns, Malone kicked open the door.

As he stepped inside the house, a slug tore a bloody path along his shoulder, before it came to rest in the door jamb. Malone quickly went to the floor, hoping the man would think he'd been hit hard.

The shooter, having been warned by his boss that Malone was coming, had been waiting in the other room. Nervously, he'd waited for Kell to enter the house. He knew that people would look at him differently, after he bagged the legendary gunman.

Upon seeing Malone go to the floor, he came rushing into the room to gloat over his victory. The fallen gunman's boots were all he could see, proof that Malone was down. He watched them for a time, to see if they revealed any trace of movement or sign of life

Failing to see the slightest twitch, a smile came to his greenish, tobacco-stained teeth. "The great Kellen Malone!" he scoffed. "Guess you weren't so tough, after all."

Longing to see the gunman's eyes closed in death, he had every plan to put another couple of bullets in Malone's body. Then, he would tell people that he shot the man down in a fair fight. That should make the saloon gals finally give him the respect he deserved.

Finally, the man could wait no longer. It was time to claim his trophy.

The triumphant outlaw stepped around the sofa, expecting to see Malone's body growing cold. He saw only the barrels of Kell's twin six-guns.

As his mind warned his body to run for cover, the guns were already belching flame. A pair of slugs ripped through his vest, leaving a couple of crimson holes, where brown tobacco stains had been earlier.

The impact knocked him over backwards, loosing the hat from his head. As Malone stood over him, the man said, "Reckon I wasn't meant to be famous."

Malone didn't respond as the man continued.

"The three of us, we had the president dead to rights at the train depot," the outlaw explained. "Then he don't show up. I even had you too, Malone."

"Yes, you did. Ought to take a little more time lining up your shot next time."

He nodded. "Since you killed me, the least you could do is share a drink," the man said.

Quickly looking around the room, Kell saw a crystal brandy decanter and some glasses beside it. He grabbed the bottle and a pair of glasses. Kneeling beside the fallen man, he poured them both a drink. Kell tossed his back in a swallow. Then he lifted the outlaw's head, and helped the man to drink his down.

"Thanks, Malone. Best drink I ever had," the man replied, before his eyes closed forever.

Casting one final glance at the end of a wasted life, Kell's thoughts quickly returned to his purpose. He moved from room to room, determined to find the man who conspired with Vincent Fielding to kill the president.

Stonegate was gone.

Frustrated by the fact that another one of the conspirators had escaped him, Malone swore softly. He started back out the front door towards his horse.

Just then, he heard a single blast from a revolver in back of the house.

Guns drawn, Malone raced around to the other side of the conspirator's home. Then he saw Gain Carson, kneeling over the dead body of Wilson Stonegate.

"He's dead," Carson said, looking up at Malone.

"I can see that. What happened?"

Just beyond Wilson's outstretched arm was a gun. His bag was there, also, indicating that Wilson had been in the process of running. A single bullet hole could be seen, only inches from the man's heart.

"You didn't think I was going to let you come over here by yourself, did you?" Gain said. "While you were dealing with those two out front, I figured Stonegate would try to go out the back way. As much as it sickened me to do it, I gave the man a chance to surrender. Glad he wasn't smart enough to take it."

As the two of them walked around the front, Carson thumbed a fresh shell in the cylinder, before holstering the gun. His horse, Cochise, followed closely behind the two men.

"I don't care what anybody says," Malone said. "That is just about the finest horse I've ever seen. Wouldn't think of selling him, would you?"

"No more than you would think of parting with Rachel."

"I was afraid of that." Suddenly, Malone's face turned serious. "How's Slate doing?"

"Doc says he has a good chance."

"I'm glad to hear that, Gain."

"Me, too. Susan would never forgive me if I let something happen to him."

As the two men rode back into town, their path took them past the railroad depot. A huge crowd of people were gathered around the gallows. The two men drew rein.

Standing on the platform was a local pastor and a stone-faced hang-man. Alongside them was a man with a black hood over his face and a noose around his neck. Although the condemned one made no statement, it was obvious that he was trembling with fear.

After reading a few brief words from Scripture, the preacher left the platform. The trap door was sprung; the man fell through.

There was a gut-wrenching thud as the rope pulled taut around the man's neck. For a few brief moments, the man kicked and thrashed around wildly, at the end of the rope. Then he went still, his body swinging from side to side in the wind.

Attorney Patrick Alexander was dead.

Kell and Gain said nothing, as they started their horses towards the hotel.

Chapter Twenty-Five

"Parties may be so long in power," Cleveland said, "and may become so arrogant and careless of the interests of the people, as to grow heedless of their responsibility to their masters. But the time comes, as certainly as death, when the people weigh them in the balance."

"So it's all over, then?" Langston said, watching the president address the crowd.

"Not quite," Kell replied. "It won't be over until Vincent Fielding is dead or captured."

"In conclusion," the president continued, "the ship of democracy, which has weathered all storms, may sink through the mutiny of those aboard. But through the events of the past couple weeks, I have recently learned an immutable truth: that honor lies in honest toil. God bless you all and may God continue to bless the United States of America."

The applause lasted for several minutes. Cleveland began shaking hands with many of those who were in front of the crowd.

"What do you plan now?" Langston shouted, trying to be heard over the noise.

"It looks like we'll be joining you on the train," Kell said, "at least as far as Denver. Joe just got a telegram from a woman. It seems Fielding's been spotted there."

"I already know that, Malone. We sent troops there. They didn't find him."

"I don't think he ever left, Langston."

"I don't know what surprises me more, Malone, Fielding still being in Denver or Clements having a woman."

"Don't let Joe hear you saying that."

"I don't intend to," Langston said, as the president waved goodbye to the crowd, and rejoined the two men.

"You don't intend to do what?" Cleveland said.

"Nothing, sir," Langston replied. "It seems that Mr. Malone believes that Vincent Fielding is still in Denver."

"That would certainly be good news if he's correct," Cleveland declared, turning his glance to Malone. "Are you sure?"

"At this point, I'm not too sure about anything, sir. But it's the best lead we have right now." Just then, an idea came to Malone. "Would it be possible, Mr. President, for you to pull the troops out of Denver?"

"To what purpose?" Langston said.

"It's clear that Fielding went into hiding as soon as he learned the troops were searching for him. Maybe he'll come back out into the open if they are gone."

"That is a brilliant strategy to capture him, Mr. Malone," Cleveland observed. "All along, I've thought you were much too smart to remain a simple rancher. Have you ever considered a career in politics?"

"I'd rather face another Cam Ellis!"

Cleveland laughed. "How is young Mr. Callfield doing?"

"He's doing fine, thanks to your Dr. Leftridge. Gain told me to thank you, if I happened to see you first."

"It was my pleasure. Frances and I cannot thank you enough for all you've done. We owe our lives to you and your friends."

"That's enough of that kind of talk," Kell replied. "Come on, Langston. I think it's time I got the president back over to the hotel."

As the two men started back over to the hotel with the president, Cleveland said, "Kell, where is Mr. Carson?"

"He's over at the doctor's office with his son-in-law."

"Do you suppose," the president asked, walking along, "that Gain really gave Wilson Stonegate a chance to hand over his guns?"

"Does it really matter if he did?" Kell said. "I'm not sure I would have. I will tell you this. I've known Gain for a long time. Never known the man to lie to me."

"He seems like a man of honor," Langston replied.

"That he does," the president said. "So you'll be joining us on the return trip, I take it?"

"Yes, I will. The job's not finished until Fielding's caught. And I won't be going alone."

"Very well," the president replied. "The more the merrier."

"If Fielding's in Denver, I'm not sure how merry it will be."

***

On the return trip from Sacramento, the president rode the train east to Cheyenne. And despite Langston's pleas for the president to continue on his way to Washington, Cleveland insisted on joining Malone and his friends, on the train bound for Denver.

The president wasn't the only one who failed to heed the advice of others. Regardless of Dr. Leftridge's wishes, and Gain's attempts to dissuade him, Slate Callfield had refused to spend another couple of days in Sacramento. The young marshal insisted that he'd been gone from Susan and his job too long already.

Gain simply muttered something about how he should have let the boy drown.

As the train approached the depot, Kell once again expressed his reservations about Cleveland's visit.

"I know I've said it before, sir, but I have to agree with Langston on this one. You shouldn't have come here."

"I told him the same thing," Frances said. "But if he doesn't listen to his wife, what makes you think you'd have any influence with him?"

Cleveland merely laughed. "We started this thing together, Kell. Is it so hard to understand that I'd want to see it through."

"No, I don't guess so," Kell said.

Anything else the two of them wanted to say was drowned out in the sound of the train whistle. The brakes came on; the locomotive began to grind to a stop.

Stirred from his slumber, Clements pushed the hat back from over his eyes. "It's about time," he muttered. "Some people may call this progress, but I won't be turning in my horse for a train ride anytime soon."

Freshly waking from his nap, Gain observed, "I have to agree with Joe. Riding around on a train, it just isn't natural."

Carson reached over and slapped his sleeping son-in-law on the shoulder with his hat. "Time to wake up, kid.

Startled by the touch, and still hurting from his injuries, Slate was instantly awake. As the young man tried to move, he winced at the pain.

"Sorry," Gain said. "Did that hurt you?"

"Did it take steel to make a railroad?" Slate muttered. "I'm not sure which of you is harder to live with, you or your daughter."

Gain looked over at the president and winked. "Grover, what is it about these kids nowadays? They gripe about everything."

Cleveland laughed.

"You mind getting the president to the hotel without me, Malone," Joe said, coming to his feet. He threw his coat over his shoulder. "I have something to do now."

Rachel giggled softly.

"And what are you laughing at?" Joe said, with a feigned look of disapproval.

"You going to see your girl?" Rachel said, softly elbowing Jesse in the ribs.

The president and everybody else in the railroad car roared with laughter. Clements saw no reason for the humor at his own expense.

"Bunch of old women and busy bodies," he grumbled, closing the door behind him.

Pausing only long enough to check his watch, Joe climbed down from the train. Then he started walking down the street towards the saloon. He pushed open the batwing doors, lingering just inside the door until his eyes adjusted to the light. Then he saw Jenny.

The sight of her made Joe's heart race.

At nearly the same moment he saw her, the redhead turned to meet his gaze. She quickly set down the tray of glasses, came rushing over, and nearly leaped into his arms.

Passionately, their lips met.

"You are a sight for sore eyes," Joe said.

"I've missed you, Joe."

Same here, Jenny. You have a few minutes to spend with me?"

"I'm going to take a break, Jeb," she said to the bartender. "Be back in a few minutes."

"Take your time, Jenny," he said. "Good to see you again, Mr. Clements."

Clements laughed. "How many times do I have to tell you? The name's Joe. If you call me Mr. Clements again, Jeb, I'll have to shoot you."

The bartender simply smiled and returned to his work.

Choosing a table in the back of the room, Clements pulled out the lady's chair and made sure she was seated first. Then he joined her at the table. About the time they sat down, Jeb brought them a couple of beers.

"Thanks, Jeb," he replied, lifting his drink.

Allowing a few moments for the bartender to go, Jenny longed to hear about his trip. She knew that Joe was never known as a particularly talkative man. But today, he seemed more silent than normal. Jenny sensed that he was distracted by something.

"What's wrong, Joe?"

"Nothing, Jenny. Just glad to see you." Taking another swallow of his beer, he looked around the room. "Have you seen Vincent Fielding since you sent me the telegram?"

Joe saw that something in the woman's eyes went cold at the mention of the name.

"There wasn't a sign of him after the soldiers came. Then they rode out of town around noon yesterday," she said. "I can't be certain, Joe. But I'm sure Fielding was outside the saloon last night, staring at me from the darkness. When I looked again, he was gone. Maybe I'm just seeing things."

Joe's green eyes locked on hers. "You looked funny when I first mentioned Fielding. Did something happen between the two of you?"

"It's been a while back, after you were gone. Fielding was waiting for me outside the saloon one night. He grabbed me and tried to make me go with him," she explained, a tear trickling down from her eye. "He wouldn't listen; he wouldn't stop. But nothing happened, Joe. Billy stopped him."

"I'll kill him!" Joe declared, his eyes turning cold. "How did Fielding take it?"

"I can't be sure that he was behind it," she explained. "But I think it was a couple of Fielding's men stopped by the saloon that night, as Billy was cleaning up. I don't think it went the way they planned it. The two of them took a real beating. Fortunately, the soldiers came the next day."

Joe said nothing as he considered the danger she had faced alone. He knew Vincent Fielding was a dangerous man. A number of men died because of his actions the past few days and weeks. And life had taught

215

him that nothing matches the vengeance of a powerful man when his actions are thwarted by the weak.

"Do you want to get out here?" he said.

Jenny blushed. "You know I can't go anywhere until my shift is over?"

"I don't mean that," he said. "Well, I do mean that…but not this time. Do you want to get out of this place? With me, I mean."

"Joe Clements," she said, with a look of bewilderment, "what in the world are you talking about?"

"I guess I'm asking you to marry me, Jenny."

Jenny knew that the lonely and troubled gunman enjoyed the time they spent together. Despite the hard and violent lifestyle that Clements led, there was a hidden gentleness to the man that she treasured. But at this point in her life, the dreams of a wide-eyed, little girl had faded into the dark realities of an aging, saloon gal. She never expected to hear those words from this man, or any other.

"Of course I'll marry you, Joe." Trying hard to restrain her excitement, Jenny reached across the table and softly touched his cheek. "But you know what I've been, Joe. Are your sure this is what you want? Are you sure I'm what you want?"

"You're the finest lady I've ever known," Joe said. "Anybody who says different will have to answer to me." He walked around the table and helped the woman to her feet. Then he took her in his arms. "I love you, Jenny."

"I love you too, Joe," the woman said, smiling. "I have to get back to work now. Will you be back later?"

"It'd take a bullet to keep me away."

"Don't say that, Joe," she scolded.

Chapter Twenty-Six

After safely getting the president to his hotel room, and still conscious of Cleveland's safety, Kell started to close the drapes on the windows. While looking through the glass at the busy Denver street, Malone saw Joe walk out of the saloon.

A big man, sitting just outside the establishment, nodded as Joe passed. Up the street, a man suddenly stepped back into the shadows, between a couple of buildings. In the man's hand, Kell saw the glint of a knife blade. Then the big man began to fall in behind Clements.

"What is it, Gain?" Rachel said.

Malone held his finger in front of his mouth to silence her. Then he gently opened the window. Earring back the hammer on his revolver, Kell waited.

About the time Clements reached the place between the buildings, the big man rushed up behind him. Kansas Jack grabbed Joe in a bear hug, pinning his arms against his side, leaving Joe unable to draw a gun. Lifting Clements off the ground, he directed him towards the ambush.

At the same time, Avery Sims charged out the shadows, planning to run the blade through Jack's helpless victim.

Coolly, Malone squeezed off a shot.

Avery Sims clutched at his chest, unsure of what happened. Staring at the bloody palm he raised in front of his face, Sims pitched over, face first in the alley.

Startled by the unexpected death of his friend, Jack momentarily released his grasp. Feeling the grip around him loosen, Clements managed to break free. Now facing the man, Joe slammed a couple of hard right hands to Jack's gut. Then he jabbed a vicious left to the man's jaw.

Kansas Jack merely smiled and backhanded the smaller man across the alley.

At the sound of gunfire, a crowd of people began to form around the alleyway. With so many innocent bystanders gathered around, Kell was unable to shoot again. But since Joe still had his gun, and the other man was making no effort to draw his, Malone was content to stand there at the window and watch the battle.

Kell was quickly joined at the windows by the others in the room.

Landing in a bag of refuse, with his head hitting the wall, Clements paused to shake away the cobwebs. Reaching down, he felt the outline of an old, solid ax handle. Joe smiled. Now it was his turn to administer a beating on the larger man.

Smiling like the weapon would have no impact on his huge frame, Jack planned to choke the life out of the scar-faced gunman. Swinging the ax handle like he was felling a tree, Clements caught the man coming in.

The blow broke a couple of the man's ribs, doubling the man over. Jack quickly recovered and rushed at Joe. But his speed was no match for the smaller man, who merely side-stepped his charge. Now behind his attacker, Joe swung the ax handle across the man's back.

Jack winced at the blow, but he kept coming.

Beginning to feel overconfident in the power the ax handle gave him, Joe caught a hard right to the jaw, a savage punch that knocked him up against the wall. Jack came at him for the final blow, when Joe slammed the handle alongside the bigger man's skull.

The blow rang like a thunderclap.

Kansas Jack stood there for a time, his head swimming in pain. A wave of unconsciousness swept over his body. Then the big man's knees buckled under him, before he fell to the ground with a thud.

Leaving Gain and Slate to stand guard over the president, Kell and Gain made their way down to the alley.

"Thanks for the help," Joe said.

Kell smiled. "Thought I might even the odds a little."

Rubbing his sore jaw and wiping the blood from his lips, Joe looked down at the body of Kansas Jack. "Him against me, you call that even?"

"I thought so, at first," Kell said, with a smirk. "Then it became clear that you were no match for the big man. Couple of times, I even thought of helping you. Didn't I, Gain?"

"Yes," Gain replied, "he stood by the window, commenting about how somebody ought to come to your aid. I, for one, was greatly touched by Malone's compassion."

"It's a good feeling to know a man can always count on his friends," Joe muttered.

Finally, the sheriff and his deputy showed up at the scene.

"Kansas Jack and Avery Sims tried to waylay this man," one of the onlookers said. "The big man over there," he added, pointing at Malone, "He shot Sims from the window. It was fair shooting, Sheriff."

"Is that how it happened?"

Kell and Joe both nodded.

"Okay, you men," the sheriff ordered, "get Sims' body out of here. The rest of you people, move along."

One of the storekeepers, curious to come and see the aftermath, handed the sheriff a bucket of water. He tossed the contents in Jack's face and the dousing stirred him back from unconsciousness.

Just then, Langston elbowed his way through the crowd. Kneeling down beside the man, he said, "My name's Jeremiah Langston. I work for President Grover Cleveland. I want to know who was responsible for sending you to ambush Mr. Clements."

The man spat in Langston's face.

Upon seeing that, the sheriff started to intercede. He held back when Kell raised his hand for the man to wait.

Langston removed a handkerchief from his pocket, pausing to wipe the spittle from his face and walrus mustache.

"I asked you who was responsible, mister. Now, before you answer, I want you to know one thing," Langston said, a look of determination on his face. "Vincent Fielding is going to the gallows for his attempts to kill the president. Do you want to hang with him?"

Kansas Jack was adamant. "I'm not telling you anything?"

Frustrated by his failure to learn the truth, Jeremiah stood to his feet and started to push his way back through the crowd. Then, he stopped. Snatching the gun from the sheriff's holster, Jeremiah started back towards the man.

"To hell with the hanging," Langston said, his thumb cocking the hammer on the revolver. The gun was still pointed at the ground, held loosely at Jeremiah's side. "If you don't tell me what I want to know, I swear I'll kill you myself. A lot of good men died because of Vincent Fielding," Jeremiah exclaimed, raising the muzzle of the gun against the side of the man's head. "Was Fielding behind this? And where can we find him? Tell me now."

Watching the scene, Clements's jaw dropped.

Kansas Jack swallowed hard. "Okay! Okay! I'll tell you, mister. But I want a promise from you, sheriff. You have to tell me that I won't swing."

The sheriff nodded. "You've got my word, Jack."

"Now get this crazy man away from me," Jack replied. "Then I'll tell you everything you want to know."

The sheriff took the gun out of Langston's hand, gently releasing the hammer. Langston stepped off to one side, taking his place alongside

Malone. Kell smiled, as he warmly slapped a big hand on Jeremiah's back.

"Now, Jack," the sheriff declared. "Start talking."

"You're right, mister. It was Fielding that told us to kill Clements," he said. "Fielding's over at the old Belson place. I can tell you that he won't come easy. The man has several gunhands with him."

The sheriff motioned at the man with his gun. "Let's go, Jack. And if you try anything, I'll give Mr. Langston the gun back."

As Jeremiah started back over to the president's room, the president's bodyguards fell in behind him. Clements looked over at Malone and Carson. "Did you see Langston?" he said, nearly in disbelief. "I might need to rethink my opinions of the man. That's pretty much the way I usually handle things."

"That's a scary thought," Kell observed, wryly. "Come on, Joe. Let's get you cleaned up. Then we've got a man to see."

***

Once in the room, nobody bothered to speak. The only sounds to be heard were guns being inspected and loaded, men preparing for battle. Seeing the others were ready to go, Kell walked over to the door.

"I'd like you to stay behind, Slate," he said. "You still can't move around real good. And someone needs to stay with the president. If they make another run at the man, then you and Langston will have to stop them again."

"You can count on me," Callfield replied.

"Me too," Jeremiah said.

Standing off to one side, while Jesse hugged his father, Rachel tried to be strong. Her eyes were filled with tears.

"Jesse needs you back, Kell. So do I," Rachel said, gently patting her belly. "The both of us do."

"Are you trying to tell me...?"

"Yes, Kell. I'm expecting a child," she explained. "Dr. Leftridge confirmed it."

Smiling at the news, Joe walked out the door, waiting for Malone in the hallway. Gain slapped Kell on the back. "Congratulations, son," he said, before joining Clements. "We'll be outside when you're ready."

Kell took Rachel in his arms, pulling her closer. Their lips melted together.

"I need to get out of here," Kell said. "We don't want Fielding to escape."

"Then go," Rachel said. "We'll be here when you get back."

"Our prayers are with you," Cleveland added.

"Be careful, Malone," Langston said.

"It ends here," Malone replied. "It ends today."

Chapter Twenty-Seven

Outside the Belson place, Tally Jenkins checked his watch.

Tally and the rest of Vincent Fielding's men were getting nervous. It had been several hours since Kansas Jack and Avery Sims went into town. They should have killed Clements by now and returned to inform Fielding. Their delay could only mean one thing: the two men had failed.

Jenkins went to talk to his boss.

"What do you want to do, Mr. Fielding? There hasn't been a sign of Jack and Avery," Jenkins said. "You could light a shuck out of here."

"There isn't time," Fielding replied. "And they would find me anyway. You'll just have to make sure you stop them."

"Okay, boss. I'll tell the men."

Fielding's gunhands were waiting for him when he came outside.

Jenkins looked at the men and said, "You need to get into position now, because they'll be coming soon. Just make sure nobody kills Malone. You understand me? He's mine."

After receiving their orders, the men scattered to their various rooftops and assorted hiding places. They were all locations that presented a good field of fire and offered some measure of cover. The men were stationed in such a way as to surround the house.

As the three riders approached the place, they came at the house from different directions. Malone would approach from the front. Gain would come in from the side. Joe would attack the house from its back.

As Gain approached the house, a pair of men exposed themselves and began firing at him. Slapping the spurs to Cochise, he put the animal into a full gallop, bearing right down on the men's position. He reined the horse at the man on the left, at the same time he fired his gun at the outlaw on the right.

Running as fast as the animal could go, his tail stretched out in the wind behind him, the horse trampled the outlaw underneath its massive body. The man's neck was broken by the force of the blow.

Upon hearing the first sounds of gunfire, Fielding calmly poured himself a glass of fine Tennessee whiskey. Turning in his desk chair, he stared at the map of the United States, that hung on the wall behind him.

Casting an eye towards the map, Vincent lifted his glass, "This one's for you, President Grover Cleveland. You've earned it."

As the man poured another drink, he took the time to fill a second glass, there on the desk beside him. Fielding had only to wait. He thought that Malone might care to share a drink with him.

He knew it wouldn't be long.

Clements raced his horse up to the house, leaping the animal over a rail fence. A man stationed on the roof opened fire. Dismounting quickly, Joe raced towards the house, bullets licking at his heels as he ran. While still on the run, Joe clipped a man taking aim on him from the window.

With Clements leaning against the side of the house, the man on the roof was unable to locate Joe's position. The outlaw feared to lean too far forward, exposing himself to gunfire.

Seeing a rock on the ground next to him, Joe flung it over to his left. The gunman on the roof turned his gun towards the sound. Just then, Joe showed himself. Firing two quick shots, he scored twice. The man toppled over to the ground below.

Long before he saw the man crouching behind it, Malone noticed the hat sticking above the top of the wagon. Malone drew rein. Pulling his rifle from the scabbard, Kell took aim at the second board below the hat. Squeezing off a careful shot, he heard the man yelp, exposing the outlaw to gunfire. Levering another round, Malone dusted the man's jacket. The man doubled over the side of the wagon, his body suspended above the ground by the waist, a trickle of blood pooling on the ground below him.

As Malone returned the rifle to its scabbard, a short man, with a tied-down gun, blocked his path. "I'm Tally Jenkins. I've been waiting for you, Malone. You know who I am?"

"Should I?"

"My uncle's name was Dotson," Tally said. "He was a guard at Yuma. I understand that you killed him."

"If you want to be accurate, you could say an arrow from the Apaches killed him," Kell said, with a smile. "But I'm plenty happy taking credit for his death. Now, if you'd care to step out of my way, I have business inside with your boss."

Jenkins was insulted by the slight. "Listen, mister. You have business with me, first."

"Well, let's get to it then," Kell said, his hand resting comfortably on his thigh. "I'm getting a little thirsty, sitting out here on this horse in the sun."

"You think all of this is funny, Malone?"

"Not really. I'm just getting a little tired of people pointing guns at me."

"That won't be a problem for you, Malone, not after today."

"I'm going to kill you in five seconds, Jenkins. Now drop your gunbelt or grab iron. Five. Four. Three…"

"Now wait just a minute."

"Two…"

"Okay, Malone. You win," Jenkins said, his eyes betraying the words he spoke. The young man went for his gun.

Malone's gun sprung to his hand in an instant, his horse moving slightly as he drew. The horse's movement caused both men's slugs to go off target.

Tally's bullet burned a path along Malone's side. The errant slug from Kell's gun caught the man in the throat.

Kell stepped down from his horse to see if there was anything he could do for the dying young man. The boy grabbed Kell's arm, trying to speak. Then he was gone.

Leaving the reins of his horse hanging, Malone started into the house. With his gun at the ready, Kell saw a man, sitting all alone at his desk in the study.

"You must be Kellen Malone," the man said. "Come on in. I am Vincent Fielding."

Sweeping the room with his eyes for any possible dangers, Kell saw none. He noticed the two glasses sitting on the desk.

"Expecting someone?"

"Just you, Malone. Care to share a drink with me?"

"Why not?" Kell replied, reaching for the extra glass.

"To your health, Malone, and that of the president," Fielding replied, as the two men tossed down their drinks.

"I must hand it to you, Malone. You played the game well. It was the first time that Cam Ellis ever failed in one of his assignments." Fielding stared at the man across from him, looking him directly in the eyes. "What happens now?"

"That depends on you."

Just then, Joe Clements entered the room. "No, Malone. That depends on me." Saying nothing further, Joe coolly palmed his gun and placed one deadly slug into the middle of Fielding's forehead.

The force of the bullet knocked the man's body backwards over his chair.

"He shouldn't have ever put his hand on Jenny," Joe muttered, reaching for the bottle. He poured the glass half full and drank it down. The empty glass, he slammed back onto the desk.

The two men said nothing as they made their way to the door. Gain Carson met them outside, after catching up their pair of horses.

"What about Fielding?" Gain said.

"He won't be joining us," Kell stated.

What happened?"

"We smote the Philistines, hip and thigh."

"Okay. That's fine," Gain muttered. "Don't answer me. But I'm dying to know which one of you was the jawbone?"

***

"So, Kell did you give any more thought to what we talked about?" Cleveland said.

"No, I don't think so, Mr. President. I think I'll stick with ranching." Malone turned his gaze towards Langston. "And thanks for considering me, Lieutenant."

"I'm disappointed to hear that," the president said. "But I respect your wishes. What about you, Joe? Are you interested in joining me?"

"I don't much care for politicians," Joe said. "But for whatever the reason, I happen to like you, Mr. President."

Cleveland threw back his head and laughed.

"Would taking the job mean that I'd have to catch a bullet for the next man to have your job, somebody I might not think was worth giving my life for?"

"That is the job," Langston replied. "After these recent events, a number of people in Washington have discussed the idea of providing round-the-clock protection for the president. We thought we would implement that plan on a part time basis, at first."

"If it's all the same, Langston, I believe I'll pass."

Dressed in their Sunday finest, the president and his friends stood outside the tiny, white, Denver church house, waiting for the parson to arrive. Joe Clements, who often faced down armed men in the street, was pacing back and forth like an expectant father. He fussed with his tie and rolled five smokes in the past ten minutes.

Langston nodded. "Despite our earlier differences, Joe, I told the president you would make an excellent choice."

"Thank you, Langston," Joe said, offering his hand. "Besides, Mr. President, the job still sounds a little too respectable for me. And Jenny has the idea that her new husband ought to spend a little time around the house for a while."

"Women are funny that way," Cleveland said, putting his arm around Slate Callfield. "So, Gain, are you interested in joining your son-in-law on my team?"

"Normally, I'd turn you down, sir" Gain said. "But after learning I'm going to be a grandfather, Nora and I don't want to be too far away from Washington. If you haven't changed your mind, I would be honored to serve the president, in any capacity you choose."

"Splendid," Cleveland said. "You won't regret that decision, Gain. And Frances and I will be honored to have you there."

For about the hundredth time in the past few minutes, Joe checked his watch. "Where is that Malone?" he muttered.

"He went to check on the parson," Gain said. "I also think he was planning to see how Rachel was getting along in getting Jenny all gussied up."

"I'd better head that way myself," the president said, before excusing himself. Cleveland paused just long enough to straighten his tie. "I have been given the honor of walking that lovely young woman down the aisle."

Langston winked at Callfield. The presidential aide spoke softly, so as not to be overheard. "Look at Clements. The man just faced down hired assassins and never flinched. Now, look at him."

Still wearing the sling around his arm, Callfield simply smiled at the remark.

Upon returning, Malone tapped Joe on the back. "Come on, Joe. Everybody's waiting for us in there. They're ready to get started."

Clements handed Malone a ring.

"You asking me to be the best man?" Kell said.

"Not really," Joe muttered. "Jenny's already getting the best man. But I figured I could trust you enough to hold the ring."

"That's mighty kind of you," Kell said "You ought to see that Jenny. She looks beautiful. You're truly a lucky man, Joe."

"I reckon so."

Malone slapped Joe on the back. "We'd better hurry up and get in there. The future Mrs. Clements is waiting for you."

"Jenny Clements, I kind of like the sound of that," Joe said. "'Til death do us part."

The End

Author's Note

Despite the fact that *Death Rides the Rail* is a work of fiction, much of what you read in the pages of this book were indeed true. It is my pleasure to briefly share some of those details with you.

While reading this book, you occasionally saw President Grover Cleveland speaking to an audience. Although many of his words were taken out of context, a great majority of the quotes attributed to him were lifted from Cleveland's own speeches.

As to my book claiming that Grover Cleveland served without a vice president for some of his time in the Oval Office, this incident was also true and has happened several other times throughout our nation's history.

As I stated in *Death Rides the Rail*, millions of acres had been acquired through fraudulent means by railroad executives, speculators, and other wealthy interests. These eighty-one million acres were returned to the public domain by President Cleveland. No doubt this action made the president extremely unpopular, as it would today with those wealthy and powerful individuals who were thwarted in their schemes.

Strangely enough, on the date of his assassination, April 14, 1865, President Abraham Lincoln signed the bill that created the Secret Service. President Cleveland was the first to receive some limited protection from the Secret Service, although the agency wouldn't be tasked with the full-time protection of the president until after President William McKinley was assassinated in 1901.

In fact, earlier in his administration, President Lincoln also signed legislation which provided the funds to build America's Transcontinental Railroad, which was the foundation for this book.

The history of the presidency, the Secret Service, and the Transcontinental Railroad are three subjects which are truly fascinating and certainly worthy of your time and attention. Those of you who devote some of your time to this reading and study will thank me later.

—R.G. Yoho

About the Author

R.G. Yoho is a West Virginia native with a passion for history and tales of the American West. Raised on a cattle farm, he is the prolific author of multiple Western novels, along with works of fiction and nonfiction. Yoho is a former president of the West Virginia Writers. Living with his wife near the banks of the Ohio River, Yoho is also a proud member of the Western Writers of America.

Coming Soon!

R.G. YOHO

BOOT HILL VALLEY

Boot Hill Valley is a funny name for a town. It's a Colorado town with a dark, brutal, and lawless past, a place which can no longer hire a marshal.

Chance McBride, one of their former lawmen, is a man who believes he has lost everything, and with nothing left to lose, he foolishly turns to the bottle. But despite Chance's drinking, he still hasn't lost the love of a good woman, his wife, Amy.

With the help of his wife and the unlikely friendship of a mysterious Arapaho, Chance reclaims his life, confronts his personal demons, and challenges the evil Ramsey brothers, who once again threaten it all.

For more information
visit: www.SpeakingVolumes.us

Now Available!

R.G. YOHO

WESTERNS

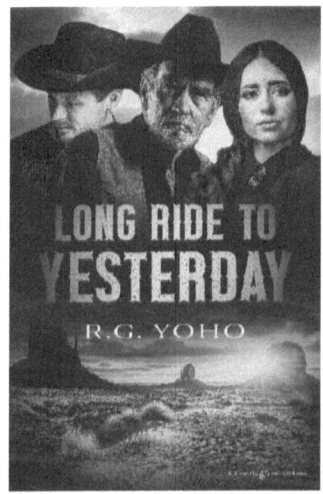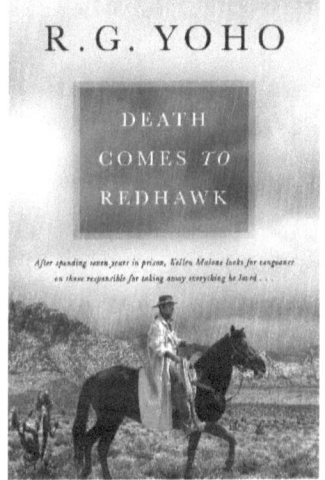

For more information
visit: www.SpeakingVolumes.us

Now Available!

SPUR AWARD-WINNING AUTHOR
JAMES D. CROWNOVER

FIVE TRAILS WEST SERIES

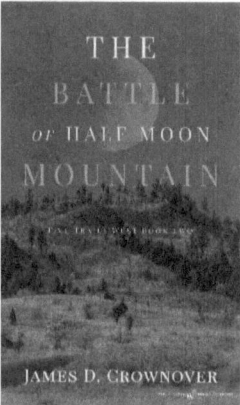

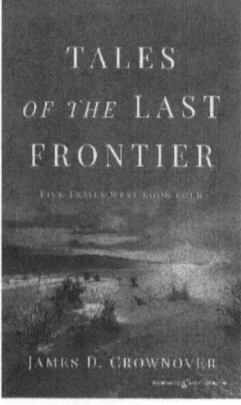

For more information
visit: www.SpeakingVolumes.us